Canoe Lady

A Novel of Artist
Frances Anne Hopkins'
Years in Canada

Books by Dot Wilson

Canoe Lady

That Orkney Girl

More books to follow...

Canoe Lady

A Novel of Artist Frances Anne Hopkins' Years in Canada

Dot Wilson

BOUNDARY LINE BOOKS

Library of Congress Control Number: 2007900303

ISBN-13: 978-0-9792407-0-6
ISBN-10: 0-9792407-0-0

Cover Design by Kathryn E. Campbell

The 37 ¢ Canadian stamp was designed by David Nethercott and issued in November, 1988. The painting by Mrs. Hopkins is titled *Canoe Manned by Voyageurs Passing a Waterfall*. Her photographic portrait is by William Notman (1863). Reproduced with permission of Canada Post Corporation.

The correct date of Frances Anne Hopkins' death is March 5, 1919.

Minnehaha Feeding Birds, Frances Ann Hopkins, oil on canvas, AV1990.32.3, Negative 58419, from Minnesota Historical Society, used by permission.

I-7335 *Mrs. Edward (Frances Anne) Hopkins as a shepherdess, Montreal, QC 1863*, from Notman Photographic Archives, McCord Museum, Montreal, used by permission.

To my grandmother, Jessie Farnell,

who sailed the North Atlantic to Canada.

To my mother, Grace Wilson,

who crossed North America from coast to coast.

And to my sister, Marianne Wright,

who retraced their journeys with me.

Contents

Acknowledgments

Writing text may be a singular occupation, but writing this book was not. It took international interest just to get me started. My friend, Irene Hunstad, wanted to know all about the artist who had done the framed reproductions on my living room walls. When I had shared the few facts I knew about Frances Anne Hopkins, Irene said simply, "Why don't you just make up the rest?" So I did, but the doing took a lot of help.

Chief among my team members were archivists Quinn Hong of the Glenbow Museum in Calgary, Alberta, and Martha Catchpole of Library and Archives Canada in Ottawa, Ontario. These art specialists escorted me into the deepest recesses of facility vaults to view originals by Frances Anne Hopkins. I thank them both for being patient with me while I swooned.

Parks Canada, both brick and mortar (or rather, log and leather), and excellent Web sites, were invaluable sources of information. Thanks to staff and volunteers at Lower Fort Garry, Selkirk, Manitoba and at The Fur Trade at Lachine, Montreal, Quebec, who gladly answered numerous questions and were ready for more.

Young volunteers Gabrielle and Amber at Saint Anne Museum in Lachine, Quebec, supplied information I used to "educate" my fictional character, Della MacLeod. In reality, the school was not built over and around Governor George Simpson's mansion until after the time period represented in my novel.

Staff and volunteers of the exceptional Canadian Canoe Museum in Peterborough, Ontario, made canoe construction seem interesting, if not easy. Thanks for the demonstrations.

Strong encouragement for this project came from Gayle Urwiller at Fort William Historical Park near Thunder Bay, Ontario. She said that it was a bit trying to correct the many visitors who insisted on calling the artist of those well-known canoe pictures "he." She felt a book was definitely needed to settle that point. Thanks, Gayle.

Also in Thunder Bay on Western Lake Superior is The Thunder Bay Art Gallery, whose staff welcomed my interest in the "Frances Anne Hopkins 1838–1919" art exhibition held there in the spring of 1990. Thank you for the fine catalog from that event which proved so helpful in detailing her drawings.

A special thanks goes to a man I met in a cemetery: Bob Smith of St. Stephen's Anglican in Lachine, Quebec. After a tour of the church the Hopkins family most probably attended, he shared with me his personal copy of that organization's history on the Lachine Canal. From that battered book, I borrowed the story of Bishop George Jehosaphat Mountain—proof that I did not make up that name!

Finally, my deepest appreciation goes to Esther Parent, Interpreter at Parks Canada Fur Trade at Lachine National Historic Site, who assisted with research, and to Barbara Fandrich, editor extraordinary, without whom every *that* would have been a *which*.

Though this work has been a group effort, whatever errors remain are mine alone.

Introduction

It is nearly impossible to study the North American fur trade, the Hudson's Bay Company, or canoe travel without encountering the artwork of Frances Anne Hopkins. This woman saw and preserved on canvas the action and color of the exciting fur trade era.

But she was a latecomer to the scene of those adventures. When she arrived on the northern bank of the St. Lawrence River in 1858, the fur trade as it had been for two hundred years was coming to a close. Fortunately, her artwork has accurately preserved a portion of the excitement.

Art essayist Robert Stacey has said that Frances Anne Hopkins "was a painter who captured something fundamental to a place, a people, and a way of life that nobody had looked at so closely or so lovingly before." Indeed, young Mrs. Hopkins' attraction to the Canadian wilderness remains evident to all who enjoy her pictures even today.

Animal pelts were valued and traded by original inhabitants of America centuries before Europeans arrived. In their search for pelts, French traders—those hearty, colorful, story-telling voyageurs we know best from this woman's paintings—explored the new continent of necessity, more than by design. With European fur-bearing animals nearly extinct, the British were not to be economically outdone. Their ships followed closely on French wakes and, by design, they established hundreds of inland routes and posts, which later would become cities. The first highways in this new world were not solid but liquid, often only a few inches above treacherous river rocks.

Using the birch bark canoe-making expertise and the stamina of the first people living along such waterways, numerous fur trading empires were established. Fortunately for today's researchers, the higher ranks of the North West Company and of the Hudson's Bay Company were heavily populated by Scots who demanded proof on paper of operation costs and profits. There was no end to this paperwork, and much of it remains on file today, from as far back as 1670.

In addition to official recordings, the majority of HBC workers—employees from the company that owned nearly a third of the area that was to become Canada—kept private journals and wrote detailed letters to family "back home." And the majority also returned to Scotland or England upon retirement, many to publish their memoirs.

Among such records are the letters and diaries of British women, wives of the higher ranking officials, that tell the trade story from another point of view. Letitia Hargrave, a wife who spent years on the southwestern shore of Hudson's Bay at York Factory, was one such. Her letters included detailed and entertaining descriptions of the people who came through her husband's post. For example, she tells of Edward Hopkins who, at age thirty-eight, married twenty-year-old Frances Anne Beechey, the future renowned artist and the namesake of this book. Mrs. Hargrave uses these words to paint an amusing picture of her first meeting with Mr. Edward Hopkins in 1842:

> He seems 23 or 24, very dandified or rather peculiar in his style of dress & uncommonly nice looking, but with a volubility of speech that I never heard equalled, & a willingness to communicate what he knows that surprised me…

Other than this observation, we have only HBC records to trace the long career of Mr. Hopkins and, through those accounts, the shadow of his second wife, Frances.

During their twelve years in Canada, the couple surely wrote to their many family members in England. Yet only three of Mrs. Hopkins' letters are known, and a museum owns one small book of canoe songs collected by Mr. Hopkins.

However, Frances Anne Hopkins left dozens of pictures from her time in Canada: pencil; pen and ink; watercolors; and oils. They have become the voice of the fur trade, but relatively few who view those scenes know that the "speaker" was a woman.

For over two decades I have wondered about her, this artist who recorded events from her life, with near-photographic exactness, on canvas. Who was she? How did this woman (who I learned had become a mother and society matron) find time in the mid-nineteenth century to oversee a household while developing an artistic career? She must have had good help!

I longed for answers to my questions, but other than scholarly works about her art (which sometimes offered a "volubility of speech" and few personal details), there were few. Thus, *Canoe Lady* came into being, to give Frances Anne Hopkins life and color, as she had done for the men of the fur trade.

I

Oh, Canada!

"Della Isobel, please fold your hands and stand still." It was not Gramma's first request, but then Gramma had a sturdy umbrella to lean on and a huge-body reason for shifting her weight from foot to foot.

They stood quietly for a long while, though others on the platform murmured pleasantly. "Do you think she will mind, Gramma Nell?" Della asked, knowing that her grandmother would wonder *mind what.* "That she has married a man who is so old?"

Mrs. Helena Gunn said nothing, keeping her stern dark eyes on the steam engine nearing the station of Lachine near Montreal, Canada. She didn't think of Chief Factor Edward Hopkins as old, though he was, in fact, nearer her own age than that of his new bride.

"This is not a thing we will talk about," Gramma Nell said finally. "You know that the boys needed a mother, and a young one will suit very well."

But would she? Mrs. Gunn wondered. The first Mrs. Hopkins—Annie Ogden Hopkins, she had better think of her now—had been born into the fur trade and had successfully reared three sons, yet she had died of a common sickness here along the St. Lawrence: cholera. Though the year was 1858, even a fine lady's lot could be difficult.

Her hands were folded and her feet rooted to the planks, but Della was swinging her long skirts from side to side. "Do you think the boys have missed me, Gramma Nell? Will they know who I am anymore?"

Mrs. Gunn was thinking yet of the new Mrs. Hopkins. Thinking that perhaps an older husband was an easier lot than wedding a young buck. Their need for each other might be more equal and maybe not so much stress would arise between them. Not that fine European people needed to do more than entertain each other and their friends. She chuckled aloud, not turning to catch the twinkle in her granddaughter's eyes.

Frances Anne Beechey Hopkins—the second Mrs. Edward Hopkins—did not know who would be waiting when she disembarked at her final destination, but *someone* would be waiting. That was the life she had been born into twenty years earlier and the marriage she had chosen to continue it. Her gloved hands rested in her velvet lap as she smiled at Nora and Millie, who were trying to contain Edward's three young children. The teacher Mr. Hopkins had hired seemed none too lively, but Frances, being a good sailor, had not until then realized that the Atlantic crossing had been a misery for him.

Well, easy was not what she had envisioned for her new life, and the first stage was nearly completed. On a riverbank not so far away was the home she would oversee. She felt completely ready. But what of the Misses LaFleur and Stapleton? Two more opposite companions she could not have chosen if she had been given opportunity.

Lenore LaFleur had been a wedding gift from the Beechey family, if a *person* can be given, or, as it were, arranged for. Miss Nora, as she was called, was a true French beauty: dark, a bit too tall and thin, but exhibiting every necessary refinement of the age. Her French was perfect, naturally, and her English charming. However, it was her abilities with a machine for sewing that were her most attractive feature. If she must be given a position title, it would be lady's maid, but Frances supposed, even before she set foot in her new domain,

2

that Nora and Millie both would end up doing a bit of many things for the household.

Millicent Stapleton, seventeen-year-old Cousin Millie, had been more a cast-off than a gift. There was no wondering, as there was with the somewhat older Nora, what possible scandal might be in Millie's background. There was simply too much of Millie to be contained by Victorian England. Her hair was too red; she had too many freckles. She was big-boned and big-hipped and, given free reign, her clothes would be too colorful. And yes, her heart was also much too soft. She loved every person and animal she had ever met and every romantic story she had ever heard.

Millie had come from the west country of England to be with Katherine Hopkins, Frances' older sister, when she had married Edward's brother. The girl had begged to be allowed to sail the Atlantic after Katherine tactfully suggested that the wilds of Canada might hold more possibilities for her than did the city of London. Everyone loved Millie, with all her *character*, especially Mr. Hopkins' dear little boys.

An excited voice saying, "Mother, Mother! Mr. Steven just said **'Thank God** we have finally arrived,'" aroused Frances from her musings. Eight-year-old Edward Gouverneur was again exhibiting his place as first-born son and calling Frances *Mother*, rather than the *Mamma* used by his younger brothers.

Frances took Gouverneur's hand very gently and said, "Mr. Steven is right, dear. We should all thank God that we have arrived safely."

Their honeymoon bedroom at Lachine had none of the elegance of any of the rooms in her mother's house back in London. Nor was it as cramped as their stateroom on the *Princess Royal* had been. Edward was already absent, as she knew business would often keep him in their future with the Hudson's Bay Company.

There was a soft tapping at the door. "Good morning, Mrs. Hopkins. I am Della, Mrs. Gunn's granddaughter. We—we are wanting to know—um—would you care for a tray, or for breakfast downstairs?"

The girl's halting English only added to her charm. Frances was looking at the loveliest creature imaginable. This is Canada! she thought instantly.

When no answer was forthcoming, the girl began again, "Would you like…"

"No, no, my dear. I will be quite happy to follow you down. Then you and your grandmother can help me meet everyone." As they moved, Frances observed a grace in the girl that she could only hope might influence Cousin Millie.

"Oh, Frances! Isn't this the most charming kitchen? It reminds me so much of home. I mean home in Devon, not London. And Mrs. Gunn has allowed me to sit here at her table so we could talk while I ate some breakfast. You don't mind, do you, Frances? I mean that I ate without you. And, well, I didn't really know where I was to sit. I hope…"

"It's quite all right, Millie. That is, if Mrs. Gunn doesn't mind your chatter." She looked with a smile toward the older woman.

"Not at all, Mrs. Hopkins. It's been too quiet here these past months. I'm only too happy to have her company. And yours, too, anytime you wish to come here."

The room was, indeed, cheery, not only due to cooking aromas, but from rays of September sunlight coming through good-sized windows set into red brick walls. A long plank table filled one end of the room, while a heavy black iron cook stove sat against the wall adjoining the formal dining room on the river side. There was one long bench and numerous bentwood chairs, and a warmth that said family.

"I wonder, Mrs. Gunn. Is this where Mr. Hopkins eats when he is home with the children?"

"It is, missus. But there's no need for you to..."

"Yes, then, I agree completely with Miss Millie. Except when society dictates, I would be most happy to enjoy meals here, with my family." Frances did not miss the smile and nod of approval of her housekeeper. Conquest number one accomplished, Mrs. Hopkins thought with pleasure.

The remainder of the day did not proceed as smoothly. While Mr. Colin Steven, the boys' tutor who had arrived from his lodgings, was pleased to join the "tour de Hopkins" as Mrs. Gunn named it, Miss LaFleur declined, thus ensuring a happy smile on the round, freckled face of her roommate, Miss Millie.

"Della and the boys are in the garden whenever you like. That girl is as able as myself to tell you the workings of a big house along the St. Lawrence. And those young ones have already inspected most of their favorite play spots." Mrs. Gunn would spare her own feet the tour.

"Young ones! How very awful of me to forget that I am the mother of three!" Frances jumped up and replaced her teacup. "Do we pass to the garden through this door?" she asked.

Della sat with two boys near her and the third standing behind them. The sun was warm, the tawny grass shiny and slick. Frances wished that she had brought her sketchbook. But there would be plenty of time for drawing pictures. And plenty of subjects.

"Good morning, Mother," Gouverneur said first, then, "Mamma, Mamma," came from Ogden and Manley, the younger boys. "Mamma, look what Della is letting us help with. Della calls them little canoes." The girl looked up with a blush.

"Sim never wants any of the sweet pea seeds to scatter, so we are harvesting the last of them." Della handed Manley, the youngest child, a chipped pottery mug so he could show the adults a treasure

5

of round, dark brown peas. Then the two older boys displayed tan pods that turned up gracefully at one end, just like the Indian canoes they had seen at the dock the day before.

Millie rescued the cup of seeds just as it was about to scatter its cargo and Frances suggested, "Shall we find this Sim person and see what he thinks of your morning's work?"

What they found first was a very large, very black hound. "Don't be afraid, Mamma. That is just Madeleine," the boys laughed.

"Madeleine," their stepmother repeated. "I've never met such a big dog. Or one with such a distinguished name. You must tell me all about her some dark winter's night."

II

Conquests

Throughout the autumn and that first crystal winter, Frances got to know her family. This was Edward's season to be at home, and he enjoyed his sons as much as his wife did.

Manley, the youngest, quickly became his stepmother's pet. At age five he was too young for Mr. Steven's classroom. Though both Millie and Della taught him his letters and read to him frequently, his Mamma was his favorite. It was on outings with Mamma that they met the Foster family, and during these outdoor times, Frances began to fill her sketchbook.

Della was their guide and source of information. She enjoyed using the English she had learned at school and was proud to share what the Sisters had taught her about the history of Lachine. "It means China, Mrs. Hopkins. Can you believe that? I am not quite sure why the explorer La Salle gave this area that name."

"Maybe Mr. LaSalle was lost," offered Ogden quietly. "Like Captain Christopher Columbus. Except Mr. Steven says that he wasn't really lost anyway."

Before the two older boys could begin a "discussion" on that topic, Frances said to Della, "Tell me more about our own destination today. We're headed beyond the usual streets, I see."

Yes, Mrs. Hopkins. I hope you don't mind. Gramma wanted some fresh greens for your dinner, so I told her I would lead us to the Foster's garden. Even this late in the season, he is sure to have something good. Mr. Foster was a black American," Della explained. "Well, he's still black, but he ran away from the southern states a long time ago, even before I was born, I think. His wife, Emma, was already here and they have worked for Mr. Hopkins and other Lachine neighbors for lots of years."

Frances gave Della's hand a squeeze on one side and Manley's the same on the other. She had noticed that a black woman came to the wash house each laundry day with a baby tied to her back. "Then the Hopkins household is fed and presentable thanks to the Fosters' help," Frances said. "What does...What is Emma's husband's name?"

"He is called Izzy, but I think he has a real name too. Maybe Isaiah. He is a farmer. We always buy the best vegetables and such from Izzy, Gramma Nell and me."

Frances hesitated a moment, then said, "Is there another way you could have worded that, Della?"

Della looked with mild alarm at this woman who had already become her idol. A little glimmer came into her eyes and she said, almost to herself, "Gramma Nell buys vegetables. I buy vegetables." Then more loudly, "Gramma Nell and *I* buy vegetables from Izzy."

The new Mrs. Hopkins was happy to find that Della's time "sitting in" at Mr. Steven's English lessons for the boys was worthwhile. They chatted happily together, but by the time they reached the farm, Frances' new outdoor boots were hurting her feet, and Della was giving Manley a horse-ride on her back.

Evenings by the parlor stove were for everyone. And every female, except Mrs. Gunn and Della, who had their own tiny cottage, spent much of the time sewing or knitting or mending. Although Frances sometimes wished fervently to work on a sketch she had made during the day, evenings were for family.

"Mother," came Gouverneur's timid voice. "Did you know that Papa has been to Hawaii?"

"Why, yes, I did, but I would like to hear more about that adventure. What can you tell me?" Over the boy's head she shared a loving smile with her husband.

"It is better if I show you," the boy said mysteriously. "Mr. Steven gave me a lesson and I have finished it today. Would you like to see it?"

Gouverneur had been only four years old when his mother died, but he may have remembered her a little. Or possibly he had blended her memory with that of his Aunt Annie, with whom the boys had stayed in London. He and Frances were both making an effort to become closer.

He has grown just in the few months we have been in Canada, Frances thought. She said aloud, "Do please show me, Gouverneur."

His proud revelation of a drawing nearly brought tears to her eyes. So well she remembered herself at this age trying to attract her father's undivided attention, not an easy task when she had four sisters attempting the same. But those girls couldn't draw like she could, and her father, being somewhat an artist himself and the son of an accomplished portrait painter, always found a moment for Frances and her pictures.

Frances suppressed the urge to offer Gouverneur immediate comment. Children could always sense undeserved praise. At least from her limited experience with children, she believed this to be true. "Why, Gouverneur, you are quite a cartographer." She used the big word intentionally. "I was expecting a picture and…Why, here you have presented a whole visual travelogue on one page." The boy beamed, as she hoped he would. "Why don't you tell me about it while Millie puts your brothers to bed."

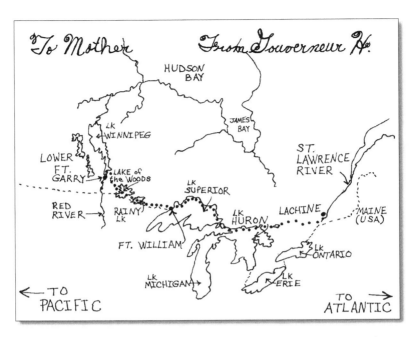

Sensitive as he was to his son's needs, Edward did not move from his chair, but did fold his newspaper with extra rustling to let Gouverneur know that he, too, was listening.

"Of course you already know that Papa is a very important man in the Hudson's Bay Company," the boy began. "And you have met Governor Simpson, the very, very most important one in Canada." Frances wondered if she could be observing the dawn of a political career. She smiled into her stepson's eyes and for the first time saw warmth there in return.

"A long, long time ago when Papa was a young man," he continued (and when I was only three years old, Frances thought to herself), "Papa went almost around the whole world with Governor Simpson because he could write in shorthand. Papa could, I mean. And Governor Simpson doesn't have very good eyes anyway and Papa got to be his secretary and that's why they became such very good friends and why Papa got to be a chief factor and everything."

Gouverneur took a much-needed breath and Frances wondered if, after all, he might actually be related to Millie.

"One boy to go," she said to Edward as they retired that evening. "The middle child, Ogden, so like myself. The misty child buried in the middle."

"My dear," her husband whispered, "do not press yourself. There will be a breakthrough."

It came in the depths of winter and quite by chance. "Now, missus. You must not worry yourself about those boys," Mrs. Gunn was saying as Frances stood frowning out a kitchen window. "The girls are keeping a good eye on them, and Sim is close by and Old Billy the woodman will likely be by today too. Why don't you just sit yourself down and have another cup of tea and work a little on your pictures." Her own mother or sister Katherine would have said nearly the same.

Though other women of her station used their parlors for morning work, Frances preferred to spend her free time in Mrs. Gunn's kitchen. Her first Canadian winter had not lacked any of the dark or cold or length about which Edward had warned her. Shortly there came a muffled pounding on the kitchen door. When Frances opened it, there stood little Ogden with the tallest, most fierce-looking "man-of-the-country" she had yet seen. "Mamma, Mamma. This is Old Billy. He's my friend, so I bringed him to Mrs. Gunn for hot tea."

While the child with his warm milk and the Canadian with his tea mug stood in the garden drinking and puffing billows of steam at each other, Frances made a little pencil sketch of the man in winter attire. His clothes were in no way more colorful than others she had seen around the town this icy winter, but he wore them so—so *comfortably*. The knee-length coat was fashioned from a famous Hudson's Bay blanket, white with fringe of green, red, yellow and black at the shoulders and hem. His hair and dark, deeply lined face were nearly covered by a hood, the whole outer garment being called a *capote*. His leggings were bright blue; his hands and feet were balls of wool covered by leather. His neck and waist were wound in bands of predominately red multicolored weaving. "This must be what a *real* voyageur looks like," she thought.

When the young ones came in for a warm-up, the drawing, which she had done on a square of paper rather than directly into her sketchbook, was still lying on the big table. Ogden saw it at once. "You made a picture of Old Billy!" he said in wonder.

"Yes," Frances replied. "I thought he looked warm and—and strong. In fact, I have decided to put Old Billy into my book with my brush and watercolors." A pause extended into the silent kitchen. "I wonder, Ogden—would you like to keep that picture of your friend for your very own?"

III

Baking Day Waltz

Della wasn't very good at waiting, especially outdoors on a February day. But cold as it was, she was waiting with special excitement because her father was coming. As they often did when Big Louie came to take guests to the governor, the two would meet for a few minutes at Mother's grave near the riverbank. Della knew that her papa would bring a gift today, because it was her thirteenth birthday.

Gramma Nell usually came along with her, to hear the news from Caughnawaga, the native village across the river from Lachine. But today she had made an excuse, saying that with it being Mrs. Hopkins' birthday as well as Della's, she had too much to do.

Della didn't exactly understand that, since Mr. and Mrs. Hopkins were to have their special celebration dinner at Governor Simpson's house on Isle Dorval. That's why Big Louie was coming across. Of course he wouldn't be in the governor's canoe this time of year, but he was still in charge of transportation.

At last she saw her father loping along the frozen riverbank and, though she knew it wasn't lady-like, she ran to meet him, throwing herself into his arms.

Louie Macleod was a big man. Some had considered him too big to be a voyageur. They said his long legs would take up too much cargo space in the birch bark canoes and that he would eat more peas and corn than he could carry. It was his future father-in-law, Morgan Gunn—Gramma Nell's dead husband—who had taken young Louie in hand, trained him as a bowsman (where there was, in fact, a little more room) and encouraged him to develop riverbank hunting skills that might add a bit of meat to the soup pot.

Della's mother had not been his first wife, nor his last. Within a year of her daughter's death from cholera, Nell had explained to Della that she now had twin brothers on the other side of the river and that she must learn to share her father with them. "It won't be so difficult to share," Gramma had said, "because there has always been enough of Louie to go around." Gramma loved to laugh!

Today, however, father was hers alone. And, as she knew he would, he reached inside his capote and drew out something gray and blue and rattling. Della gasped with pleasure.

"Lower your head, *ma petite*," Louie said, "and I'll drop this trinket over."

Even for the second or so it took to accomplish this, Della hated to take her eyes off the shell and bead necklace. She had seen none other like it.

"It is so beautiful, Papa. Where does it come from? We don't have such shells here, nor do we use so many blue beads."

Louie pulled her heavy black braid around to her chest and laid it just to the side of the oval-shaped gray shells that made a square mat under her chin.

"This was my mother's. Your *grandpere* brought it back all the way from the Pacific coast when he took Governor Simpson there many, many years ago. Before she died, my mother said that one day I would have a daughter and this should be passed on to her. Today is that day, *ma petite*."

Della hugged his neck again and he kissed her on both cheeks, the way his French ancestors had done. "I must go now, as I see my passengers coming along. I will send word to Nell when I can stop again." And he ran off as quickly as he had come.

Della stood much longer than was wise, watching Mrs. Hopkins in a fine party dress with very wide hoops and Mr. Hopkins in a tall beaver-felt hat and dark cloak board the sleigh to be driven across the frozen river toward Isle Dorval. She thought to herself that she was so lucky to have Big Louie as Papa, and that he was not just a birthday father. For it was Louie who paid for her to be taught by the wonderful Sisters of Saint Anne.

Though she didn't want this moment to end, she did want to show Gramma the necklace, and she needed to move after standing so long in one place. So back she scampered to the warmth of the Hopkins' kitchen, where her grandmother should be free now that Mr. and Mrs. Hopkins had departed.

The windows were steamed from cooking and there appeared to be more than one moving body inside. Della opened the outer door cautiously and heard loud laughter and voices behind the inner door. She removed her fur muff, hung her wool hat, gloves, and cape on a peg, and removed her heavy outer shoes. Then she slipped into a pair of house shoes and entered the kitchen. The plank table was surrounded by people: the Misses LaFleur and Stapleton, Mr. Steven, the three Hopkins boys, and Sim, all smiling at her in expectation.

"Happy Birthday, Della!" they all shouted.

It was the first party she had ever had. "A might special day now that you are a young lady," Gramma Nell said. The boys, with help from Millie, had made paper chains to place on her head and around her neck. It was then that everyone saw her father's gift.

"And what might we have here?" asked Sim, his sharp eyes, old that they were, never missing something new. A suitor is it? And me all this time thinkin' you was my girl." He made a sad face while all the others laughed with glee.

Their merrymaking lasted until past dark, which wasn't so early now that the worst part of winter had passed. And because she *was* becoming a young lady, Della did not fail to notice the competition between Miss Nora and Miss Millie for the attention of Mr. Steven. Nora would "slip" and call him Colin, but neither Millie nor Della would ever have been so bold. "We will not be having seven courses, as those at the big house will eat today. We here will be having seven *desserts!*" Everyone around the table clapped their hands at Mrs. Gunn's announcement and Della wondered how her grandmother had managed to keep so much good food a secret.

Sometimes when Millie came to Gramma's cottage for an evening chat—uppity Miss Nora never came—she and Della would discuss Mr. Steven. That is, Millie would present all the latest news about him: Mr. Hopkins was well pleased with his tutorial; young Mr. G. followed around behind his teacher and copied his every move. When Millie said that she hoped there would be lots more Hopkins boys for Mr. Steven to teach, Gramma ended the subject by saying firmly that God would be deciding that and, therefore, they need not concern themselves with it.

Della felt quite grown up when just she and Miss Millie took Sunday walks together the following spring. Millie always had such interesting things to say, and because of her "station," someplace between these company folks and the people across the river, Della didn't talk with many other girls her age outside of her classroom.

On a Sunday in late April, after Millie had returned from St. Stephen's Anglican Church service with the family and after Della had come from the Roman Catholic mass with the Sisters, they had helped Mrs. Gunn with dinner preparations. Promising to be no longer than an hour, they then began a walk along the riverbank.

"Della, my friend," Millie began. "You wouldn't believe the stories I've been hearing from our stuffy Nora about The Little Emperor."

Della became a bit uncomfortable. She was never allowed to call Governor Simpson by that nickname, even though he did rule the company like—well, like an emperor—and even though he was, at full height, not more than an inch taller than the girl herself.

"Is this something that Gramma would want me to hear?" Della asked timidly, mainly by way of not having to feel guilty later.

"That I wouldn't know, but it's time you began to learn about life. With only a granny and an absent papa to guide you, you are never going to catch up with your body."

Della picked up a few pebbles and then tossed them all at once into the recently ice-free water. She sat herself down on a large rock, by way of invitation for Millie to continue.

"Do you *know* how many bastard children that little man *has*?" Millie began.

Della gasped and turned her red face away. But she didn't stop listening.

"I don't know if I even got them all. Nora mutters so and her accent is so much more noticeable when we're dropping off to sleep. And probably no one should believe the gossip of those seamstresses who meet every week down by the yacht club. They are such old biddies. Oh, I hate having to share a room with her! But she does tell good stories. Well, interesting, at least."

Della turned back to look at Millie, but the older girl was gazing over the river toward Caughnawaga, seeming to talk more to herself than a listener.

"Nora said there are two daughters back in Scotland which Governor Simpson actually acknowledged before he ever joined the company.

She says the governor himself is a bastard, though it was his *father* who kept him."

Della knew that she shouldn't be hearing any more, but she didn't leave her seat as she should have done.

"Now, this part is pretty much for sure, because there are just too many women "of the country" who know the details. The little governor has at the very least five other children by four women here in North America. And all *before* he was ever married to poor Lady Simpson or was made a Knight of the Realm by our good Queen Victoria!"

"We had better start back," Millie said in the middle of her local history account. "No wonder Lady Frances Simpson preferred to live away from her husband back in England for a long while. And no wonder she died after so many babies in such a short time when she did finally come back here. And now that little man, for all his activity, is left with only one white son to follow in his footsteps. What a wild country this is, don't you think, Della?"

It was many weeks before Della could approach her grandmother with the questions which had troubled her since that springtime walk with Millie. There had been a time, especially after her mamma died, when she and Gramma could cozy themselves in their cottage and talk about anything. But, in comparison to what she wanted to know now, those subjects were totally childish. Yet there was no one else that she could turn to, certainly not her father.

The kitchen door stood open to allow summer breezes into the hot room. Mrs. Hopkins, formerly so active, was finding it necessary to spend much of each day on the veranda with her feet on a stool. The younger boys were there now too, so it was a safe time for Della to talk privately while they worked. Mrs. Gunn was struggling to hold a huge shallow wooden bowl with one hand and turn out the day's bread dough with the other. Della blurted out, "Gramma, am I a bastard?"

"Good lord, child! Where did that come from?" But Nell Gunn had an idea who had planted such a seed and she saw the need to answer. "No, my darling, *you* aren't a bastard, but by present calculations, I am."

Della's mouth and eyes went round at the same moment. She should have known not to open such a topic—ever!

"Now, don't look like that, my sweet. This is as good a time as any to teach you a lesson about our people. It isn't just those holy Sisters, or Mr. Steven either, who know a thing or two." Nell slammed down a huge ball of dough and began the laborious process of kneading it smooth.

"Truth be told," she continued, "half the population of this land is bastards, if we apply the white peoples' thinking. But that's exactly what the governor wanted, back when he came here—when was that now, maybe 1820s?"

Della's young hands began to pinch off and roll small lumps of dough into dinner buns. She knew that Gramma was looking at her, but she kept her eyes on her work.

"You see, the governor figured that the best way to get the best furs was to marry—oh, all right, let's say—to form, hmm—I think it was called "connubial alliances" with our people who had the best trapping lands. What a name for something so natural! *Connubial alliances* indeed! That was what the early voyageurs did anyway. So the governor just encouraged them, especially the clerks and small post factors, to be, well, I suppose you could say, more—" she began to chuckle deep in her mound of belly, "to be more *economically selective* about their women friends." Now she laughed outright. "No one ever doubted that the company's new governor was out to make lots of money for the business and, thereby, for hisself."

Nell set a dish of soft butter before Della, patted the girl's shoulder with a flour-dusted hand, and motioned that she should coat with the butter the brown tops of a tray of buns fresh from the big oven.

"Now, for what you're really wantin' ta know. The company gave my mamma to your great-grandpa when she was fourteen years old. She traveled the canoe routes with him—sometimes with some of us young ones. Yes, you've heard those stories before. It's just that nobody ever bothered to say that nobody ever took the time to marry the old folks in a church, or anywhere else." Nell sighed, wiped her sweating forehead with her apron and continued. "When my papa's contract was up, he went back home to Scotland, well, Orkney—same thing—and gave Mamma and all us kids to his friend, Mr. Wallis. He's the one I remember best, because it was him who found Mr. Gunn for me to marry. But by that time the company at least *asked* me if I wanted to go away with Mr. Gunn. I was fourteen and a woman by then, so I figured your grandpa was as good as the next. When the end came of his company days, he turned out to be even better because he chose to stay right here with me and your mamma and her brothers when he retired. A good man, my Morgan Gunn."

They had been moving around the kitchen in what Della thought of as The Baking Day Waltz. Della had remained quiet so as not to interrupt Gramma in a story that she seemed to enjoy telling. "So, when it came time for your mamma to be someone's woman, the system had changed a bit. Women of our people were valued for their beauty, which came, I believe, from all that mixing of French and Scots and English and different North American people's blood. And they were also valued for their strength and knowledge about the fur business.

"Your grandpa and I thought we might never get rid of our only daughter, our beauty Isobel." A sigh. "Our Belle would not take this man or that man who offered. Some of them even said they would marry her in whichever church she wanted. But no."

"My mamma waited a long time for my Papa Louie, didn't she, Gramma?" Della finally spoke.

"Honey, she was near to sixteen before that giant came and swept her into his best canoe and ran the Lachine rapids with her. And it was the same Father Kelly you know from Saint Anne who married them. The only wife Big Louie married in any church. I'm surprised you didn't know all this a long time ago. Now let's set us down for a cup of tea. Here. Take this cup first to Mrs. Hopkins."

"With pleasure," Della said, giving her grandmother a big hug.

IV

In Stitches

Mrs. Hopkins didn't show feelings for her family in a physical way like Della's Gramma and Papa did. Yes, she coddled little Manley, but she seemed to reserve her touching for brush to canvas, and no one could fault her in that regard. Most of the time Mrs. Hopkins just drew with a pencil or sketched with pen and ink. She always had her sketchbook with her. Della thought she drew pictures because she missed her own mama across the ocean. This way she could at least send pictures to her mama.

Since there wasn't a good place indoors to use as a studio (though the far end of the kitchen was pressed into service from time to time, leaving just the hint of oil scent when she was using that rather than watercolors), Mrs. Hopkins made many of her pictures outdoors and didn't mind when she had one or more on-lookers. Manley naturally was the most frequent, but by the autumn of 1859 he, too, was in Mr. Steven's upstairs schoolroom. Mr. Hopkins had instructed his housekeeper to see to it that Mrs. Hopkins always had one of the young ladies with her while she was "in a delicate condition," so it was Della who walked with her a little each day and sat with the mother-to-be when her rounding body demanded a rest.

Mrs. Hopkins was a great one for walking, and exercise was quite acceptable for upper-class British ladies. They walked along the Lachine canal toward Montreal, to the train station, through the European people's cemetery at St. Stephens, and often they strolled as far out as the farms of Izzy and his neighbors. Miss Nora had been quite talented at designing costumes which cleverly concealed "the condition." During the day Mrs. Hopkins often wore a wrapper: a long, lightweight robe that fell straight from her shoulders, which Nora had designed with elbow-length sleeves so as not to impede her art work. When Mr. Hopkins was at home in the evening, Frances wore what Nora termed "sacque and petticoat." These were really just a full skirt that tied under her arms and a short, open jacket with a big bow under her chin. In the case of young Mrs. Hopkins, however, such altered dress was not necessary until nearly the lying-in time.

Mr. Hopkins, always busy in the service of Governor Simpson and very often traveling throughout the district in his company, encouraged his young wife to exercise for her health and for that of the coming baby. And he encouraged the drawing, which she did for her own entertainment. Months earlier, on her very first visit to the governor's manor, Edward had proudly shown Frances several pictures that painter Paul Kane had done at the request of Governor Simpson.

"You understand by now, my dear, that the fur trade is changing. Has, indeed, changed already from mainly beaver and other animal pelts to food stuffs and, well, to any commodity which we—or I should rightly say, the governor—think will bring profits to the company. On the Pacific coast, we have an operation north of the Columbia River at Nisqually set up specifically to produce farm crops, and those aren't all shipped back to England anymore. We sell to nearly anyone who has the ready price, even the Russians."

Unlike the majority of British wives she had met in North America, Frances was sincerely interested when her husband talked about his work. But it was his eldest son, Gouverneur, and those lovely paintings of the western lands by Mr. Kane, that gave direction to the twelve years she was to spend in Canada.

"Mother and Father," Gouverneur began very formally, "as you know, I am sure, it will soon be time for Ogden and me to attend school in England."

"And I will be so happy to see Aunt Annie and Aunt Katherine and all the cousins again," said Ogden before his brother silenced him with a look.

"Your eldest pupil is becoming quite a young man," Edward whispered to Mr. Steven, who sat with the proud parents in the front parlor. "You have our appreciation, Mr. Steven."

His son was ready to begin his presentation. "Mr. Steven was disappointed when he first came to Canada because he thought everybody still traveled around by canoe. But we have a fine canal between Montreal and Lachine, and we have many rail lines, and we have steamboats which can go to the places where my father and Governor Simpson used to go only by canoe." Gouverneur took a deep breath and glanced at the paper crumpled in his hands.

"Mr. Steven has asked the men he lives with in the bachelors' quarters to tell him stories about the long-ago times. Sometimes I even got to go there with him to listen to them talk, only he wouldn't allow them to drink when I was there."

His stepmother swallowed a snicker, but quickly recovered. She, too, was interested in those stories of the past. She, too, had been disappointed that the way of life she had expected to find along the St. Lawrence River and through the trade routes of the western lakes was fading so quickly into history.

"Because I think it would be very good to become a cartographer, I am not going to say any stories, but I am going to show you my maps of the trade routes. They are still there—the old trails and portages and early people, who I am going to call North American people. Real voyageurs—even like Big Louie—still use the old routes sometimes."

He turned toward his stepmother. "I'll show you my drawings in a moment, Mother. First I want to tell you about something else I heard the men talking about in the Old Stone Warehouse." Gouverneur cleared his throat, shifted on both feet and took another breath. "Of course you know that the queen, that is, Her Majesty Queen Victoria, has chosen Ottawa as the capital city for the Province of Canada. One old man—oh, I'm sorry, Mr. Steven. One *gentleman* who had lived in Halifax a long time ago said that the queen likes Canada a lot because her papa—her *father* lived here for so long that people began to call him Canada's resident prince." He waited for the expected smiles.

"Her father—oh, I've forgotten his name, Mr. Steven. Maybe William? Well, it doesn't matter, because he did what the church would call *good works* for the people. I'll tell you some of them: made new barracks for the troops; had better roads built; set up a telegraph system. That's some of them. Oh, yes. I also forgot the best ones: Saint George's church and the clock tower. Maybe there were some others also, but what I really want to tell is that his daughter, our queen, is also going to do good works and have a fine building made in Ottawa. This will be the Parliament Building and someone from the Royal Family will come here to put the most important stone in the building. The old gentleman from Halifax explained that the royal person who comes to lay the stone—he said he was quite sure it will not be the queen because Her Majesty is no spring chicken…" (Again, a wait for the smiles, except from Mr. Steven.) "He said that the royal person doesn't actually carry the stone or anything. They just say some words over it. But we don't know yet who that royal person will be."

"And do you know what else, Mother?" (Gouverneur was obviously straying from his script, Frances could tell from Mr. Steven's unease.) "It's a rule that the company must give two black beaver pelts and two elk skins to whoever comes from the monarch's family.

Isn't that right, Father?" Edward nodded, with a broad smile.

"Now, the most exciting part and the end of my lesson: The men said that already Governor Simpson is planning a beat-all celebration for whoever comes to lay the stone, because, of course, that person will be entertained *royally* by The Honorable Company.

"So, my next lesson will be about watching the new canoes for the celebration being built over at Caughnawaga. And, Mother, Mr. Steven and I would like to invite you to come along when we go 'into the field' as Mr. Steven calls it, even if there aren't so many fields over there now."

Frances was delighted, both with the boy's report and with the invitation. The only thing that might keep her from accompanying them would be the baby she was carrying.

She and Edward shook the boy's hand and assured Ogden and Manley that, yes, if all could be arranged, they too were included in Gouverneur's invitation "into the field."

The household baby linen was well-used and yellowing, reported Mrs. Gunn and besides, she had hinted to her employer, Mrs. Hopkins should have every article brand new for her first baby. In private, she had huffed to her assistants, "Isn't it just like the fine Beechey sisters to send across ruffles and frills instead of the much more necessary dailies!" So off went both Nora and Millie to the company store.

Mademoiselle LaFleur was, indeed, an incredible seamstress, for the exact reason that she did no seaming by hand. How she had come to own the only sewing machine in the village of Lachine was a story thankfully unknown to her Victorian employers. Nor had she shared the details with Miss Millie. She was tempted to do so as they walked along Front Street toward the dry goods counter of the Hudson's Bay Store—the counter which now used the European designation dry goods *"department."*

Back in the year 1855, three years before Nora had come to work for the six Beechey ladies in the home of the famous Admiral Frederick Beechey, explorer, she had attended the Paris World's Fair with her Scottish mother and French bank clerk father. Her father had won the prize offered by a newly established business from The United States of America called the Singer Company.

The LaFleur family was not wealthy, and though they were proud of their prize, (which the doting father had given to his only daughter), they had no funds to spend teaching her how to use the machine, even if someone could be found to do so. But young Lenore was resourceful. On her own she located the American man who had demonstrated the machine's wonders to the World's Fair crowds. His name was Arnold, and it had not taken long for lovely Mademoiselle LaFleur to work out an exchange for sewing lessons. The instruction had been arranged to occur while both her parents were out, not easy to manage and, as fate would demonstrate, not wise for the girl's future. Her father soon became suspicious.

Her once passive father would not listen to Lenore's story about attempting to better herself. He considered what she had done quite the opposite. He threw both Lenore and the offending machine into the street—literally. Only through the financial assistance of her married lover, Arnold, had the girl been able to make her way to London and the fashionable ladies of Beechey House.

"Ah, my friend," Nora sighed to Millie these many years later. "It will be a pleasure to work on fine white linen and soft baby flannel. I become so very tired with little boys' shirts and one fine gown after another." Millie wasn't really listening. She had supposed that Mr. Steven was with the boys in their classroom. But there he stood just down the street, chatting with two company clerks. Millie had seen the young men in the village now and again. She smiled her prettiest, and all three men tipped their beaver hats, but their eyes were on Miss Nora, not on her.

"That's my fate," Millie said, "to be always in company with someone as pretty as you."

Nora, more animated than usual, said lightly, "It is not such a bad-awful fate, I can tell you, Mademoiselle Millie. Come along, then. I think, along with the white fabric for the baby, we should also purchase a new ribbon for your green church dress."

V

Into the Field

Edward thought it was too soon after the birth of her first child for an outdoor excursion, but his young wife was such an adventurous woman. "The outing will be good for her," Mrs. Gunn had whispered. And her employer had to admit that both Frances and his fourth son seemed in excellent health. Not that the baby would be going along, of course. He would remain in Lachine with the wet nurse his mother had employed for him at the suggestion of the wife of another company officer.

It was spring again, and if Edward were to ask Mr. Steven and the boys to wait much longer, the canoes would be finished or he would be away on post inspections with the governor. No, today would have to be "canoe day."

"Now, Della," Mrs. Gunn cautioned, "you stay close to the lady and let Miss Millie look to those boys. I do think Mrs. Hopkins is as excited as they are, and we don't want her stumbling over the clutter there in the village."

Gramma Nell had allowed Della to go twice with Mrs. Hopkins to Governor Simpson's island house. Though he had not been at home on one of these occasions, he had encouraged the wife of his favorite employee to visit as often as she wished to study Mr. Paul Kane's paintings. Mrs. McGuire, known as "Old Maud," Governor Simpson's housekeeper, had quite the stories to tell of herself sitting and watching "the little blond lady" as she called Mrs. Hopkins, while the little lady sat and studied each of those pictures in turn.

"That lass looked for so long at the picture they call *Brigade of Boats* that I believe if she could, she would have jumped right into it, along with all those sails on that choppy Saskatchewan River." When the two housekeepers were leaving the center market, Old Maud turned to add, "And you know what else she did, Nell? Why, she sat right down on the front grass with your Della and she made a picture of Mr. Simpson's little house. Can you believe that?"

Today, on their trip across the St. Lawrence, that "lass" would get her fill of canoes. More than she could ever remember, Mrs. Gunn thought.

There were eight in the party: the Hopkins family, plus Della, Millie, and Mr. Steven. Big Louie had said his men would hold a fish fry for their guests, but Mrs. Gunn insisted on sending along two large baskets of *her* cooking too. She waved them all goodbye from the veranda. She didn't know where that stuffy Miss Nora had gone to, but thought that for once having just the nurse and baby left in the house would be a pleasure.

Della was immensely proud when her papa handed her into his canoe just as he had done the real ladies. There were cushions to sit on and colorful trade blankets to protect their dresses from any splashes. "Don't fret, Della," her seat partner, Millie, told her as the men draped the blankets over them, "you'll get plenty of opportunity to show off your new dress when we get there."

Miss Millie and Mrs. Hopkins were wearing old gowns without hoops, but Della couldn't resist showing her father the sky blue dress she had helped to sew. Miss Nora had designed it especially for her in the color that, the seamstress had said, would best complement her pretty skin and her unusual necklace.

Nice as the dress was when she had the first fitting, Della had said, "Even with the necklace, it seems, well, I'm sorry to say, Miss Nora, it seems rather—well, not very colorful."

"I supposed you might think that, petite mademoiselle, so look what I have for you." Onto the table of her tiny attic workroom, Nora poured a basketful of fabric scraps. Della recognized pieces from every item Miss Nora had constructed since her arrival and possibly some bits left over from when the first Mrs. Hopkins was alive.

"Oh, but how can we use such little bits?" Della asked.

"Of course, *you* will put them together into a long ribbon and then *you* will sew them onto the bottom of your gown, just as I do for Mrs. Hopkins. Three, maybe four bands of colors all joined together by *you* on my sewing machine."

Della could hardly believe her ears. "You will teach me to use the machine?" she asked.

"But who else will use it one day when I am gone?" Nora asked in return. "Millie is only good for putting a hem in squares for the baby's bottom." They laughed together at the thought of Millie's domestic struggles.

So it had come about that beneath the blanket that now protected the blue dress were three bands of patchwork and two triangular neckerchiefs sewn, not without a few struggles of her own, by a proud Della Macleod.

The picnic guests, save for Mrs. Hopkins and Millie, had been across before to Caughnawaga, but the village looked (and smelled) different, depending on the season. There were numerous columns of smoke drifting into the morning sky and centers of activity all along the riverbank.

While the *milieux*, the men who paddled from the middle seats of the canoe, removed all the picnic cargo to an area with logs and stumps surrounding a low-burning fire, Mr. Steven and Gouverneur began the tour. Mrs. Hopkins walked arm-in-arm with her husband, and Della and Millie each took a younger boy's hand, much to the boys' disappointment.

All her life Della had known about canoes, but until today she had not realized how much there was to be known. She listened rather distantly as first Gouverneur then Mr. Steven and even her father explained what the workers had been doing during the past months.

Gouverneur: "The canoes you have been in most often, Mother, are called *Canot du Maitre*, or Montreal canoes. They are used mainly on calmer waters, like lakes. But if there are many people to take at once, like we were today, they can be used on the river too."

Mr. Steven: "I'm afraid we're going to mix a lot of things together in our explanations, Mrs. Hopkins. You see, the region of the country the canoe is made in and its purpose determine what is used in its construction. While all of them are, indeed, made of the rind, or bark, of the birch tree, and while the inner frame is of cedar, the various parts can be stitched together with split larch or spruce root, the same as you may see used in some basket making."

Della looked at Mr. Steven as though seeing him for the first time. He had such a nice voice—deep and so pleasantly Scottish.

Gouverneur: "Did you notice, Mother, that the birch bark is put on inside out? I mean, the part that held it tight to the tree trunk is what will now touch the water."

Although Della and Millie were showing only polite interest, Frances was fascinated. "And what is it, Gouverneur, that the men are cooking which smells so especially good?" the honored guest asked.

"Fortunately, it isn't our lunch," the boy laughed.

"It's pitch, Mamma. That sticky stuff that drips out of trees and won't come off when I get it on my hands." This was Ogden's contribution and for once did not annoy his older brother.

Gouverneur: "The resin they use can be from spruce or from pine trees. But it has to be melted down and made thin enough to coat the seams so they won't leak. Bear grease and charcoal are added to make it strong and give it the black color."

"I have most pleasant memories of evenings around a fragrant riverside campfire watching the men mend a canoe for the morning's journey," Edward told his wife. "The very smell puts me in mind of any number of songs they sang at that work, as well as those they sang when they were paddling on the water."

There was more to be told about the intricate process of canoe making, but at that point Big Louie came quietly to Della's side and said, "You look very pretty, daughter. Marie will bring your brothers to water's edge just before we go across again."

The group continued to wander among canoes that were in all stages of completion. Each boy got to add some melted glue or fit a stitch through a hole. But Frances had the most fun of all. She was handed a wooden bowl of red paint and a beaver-hair brush and allowed to add the final touch to a round emblem on the bow of a majestic craft.

"It won't bring bad luck, will it?" she turned to ask her husband. Edward indicated that Big Louie should answer.

"Not a bit, madame. Iroquois women help in many ways with the canoe making. The women say that is the reason the craft is so strong." Louie smiled happily and flashed his dark eyes at all around him.

* * *

Della did not mind that the twins' mother pushed her boys forward, then removed herself farther along the water's edge. Bobby and Johnny ran gladly toward their sister and were wrapped tightly into one loving arm each.

"My, so big you are!" Della said, as she always did at the start of each visit. When they had been younger the boys had been shy with her, but now they accepted her visits as a very special part of their life.

"A story, Della!" they chorused. "Tell us a story!"

"I'm afraid I don't have much time today," she said sadly. "You can see that the people are nearly finished with their picnic. But look what I have brought for you." From the pockets on each side of her dress she took a golden brown wheat bun and gave one to each smiling child. "These are for the grandsons of Sky Woman—the Maker of Twins," she said solemnly.

When the food was finished, Della said gaily, "And these are from Sister of Twins." She tied a kerchief around each boy's neck and kissed them soundly on both cheeks. It was Johnny who noticed first that the colors of their scarves matched the trim on Della's dress.

"Now you are a twin with us!" Johnny said.

Bobby answered in disgust, "There can't be *three* twins, Johnny. Sky Woman made only two—the good one and the bad one. And I'm the good one!" He hit his brother's arm playfully and was chased round and round Della's skirts.

"Stop! Stop!" Della laughed. "I have to go now. See, our papa is signaling to me." The boys threw themselves into her arms and simultaneously kissed her on her cheeks.

On the crossing back to Lachine, Millie said to all, "It's a good thing the People do build such sturdy cargo craft. After all the fish and other treats I ate at our picnic, this boat needs to be strong!"

Mrs. Hopkins just shook her head and smiled. Della's thoughts were on the few moments she had had with her little brothers. They were strong boys at just under six years old, already showing that they would be tall like their papa. François John and Dominic Robert the twins had been named, but Papa didn't mind that she, as the English would do, called them Johnny and Bobby.

True, she had gotten the hem of her new dress all dirty when she had leaned down to tie a kerchief around the neck of each boy, but she and Emma could remedy that next washday. Della had sewn together different scraps of fabric to make a distinctive gift for each of her brothers. She hoped that if they wore their kerchiefs when she visited, which wasn't often, she would be better able to tell Bobby from Johnny.

VI

A Strenuous Visit

Frances sat in the boys' room rocking baby Raymond while Edward talked to his sons about the inspection trip he would begin with Governor Simpson at daybreak. She disliked so for them to be parted. That was why her sister, who the boys called Aunt Bette, had come to be with them for the summer.

Edward was telling the story of the Hudson's Bay blanket, which had become nearly as much a symbol of the company by 1860 as beaver pelts had been a century earlier. "Do you know what standardization means?" he asked the boys, but looked at Gouverneur.

"I could offer a supposition," the big brother said, and Frances smiled into the face of her sleeping infant, hoping that he would remain a baby for a long time.

Gouverneur continued, "…that all the blankets will be made the same from now on." The boy considered his answer a moment. "No. No, that could not be right, Papa, because everybody knows we have white chiefs' blankets and blue and red and green ones, so it couldn't mean that."

"But you were thinking in the right direction," Edward encouraged, and Frances thought again how very fortunate she had been to marry such a kind husband and devoted father.

Edward continued, taking the edge of Ogden's "chief's blanket" in his hand and showing the small indigo lines on its lower edge. "It has been decided that every blanket of a certain size and weight will now have the same points, or marks, on its edge."

"But I thought those marks were for how many beaver pelts you must trade," Ogden said, sounding quite disappointed.

"No, son. They never had such meaning, though you are not the only one who was somehow misled," he said kindly.

Frances moved quietly into the nursery, the room that had been Manley's two years ago when she arrived, and placed the sleeping baby in his little bed. Edward would join her and Bette only after taking his boys on a "blanket tour" to the Oxfordshire and Yorkshire factories where the wools were worked. Maybe he would even tell them about the Pacific coast native people who valued the item so highly that stacks of wool blankets rather than pelts were now a sign of wealth.

Bette, Millie, and Nora sat in the lingering evening light, each with her handwork. Millie knitted or mended stockings continuously, Nora was making something frilly and lacy again, and Bette had various pale colors of embroidery thread spread on the arm of her chair. Bette was blond, like her sister, but in an almost faded version. She had arrived from England not only to be a companion for the new mother during the long months that Edward would be away, but also for the excitement of the royal visit, which would take place in late August. Bette had brought yards and yards of delicate fabric and the latest fashion books along so that Miss Nora could turn the Beechey sisters into regal hostesses for the celebration. Even now, months before the actual event, there was talk of little other than the festivities.

This night Frances grew tired of their chatter and she was glad, shortly after Edward's arrival, that the three women excused themselves and retired. Edward looked tired and worried. Perhaps it was just that the long beard he wore made him seem a bit dark and old.

"What is it, dear?" she asked. "The boys?"

36

"No. They are wonderful," he said. But there was certainly something troubling him.

"It's the governor," he said at last. Frances turned to him frowning.

"Is Governor Simpson not well, Edward? He seems to me always so vigorous."

"That may be part of the problem," her husband said, a frown now creasing his own forehead. "He has always done everything to excess, and as fast as it could possibly be done. These preparations for the prince's visit are to the greatest extent under his *personal* direction. He is no longer the young man he was when he took over the governorship. Tomorrow he will begin a grueling inspection tour, *tired*. And he will return even more fatigued."

"My dear, can't you…"

"You are aware that he listens to no one. You know there is only one way to proceed: *his* way. We who are nearest him do as much as we are able to cushion his life, but he allows very little. It has been the same since I have known him these—how many, twenty?—years."

She said no more. There were more pleasant ways to spend their last hours before his long absence.

* * *

The four young women spent time on the veranda nearly every day that summer. Often Mrs. Hopkins entertained her lady friends of the company or the government at tea. Then Millie and Della (rarely Nora) would serve while Bette joined her sister in visiting with the guests. More often, however, the porch would ring with children's laughter, an occasional baby's cry, or the soft singing of Emma when she came by from the washhouse to sit in the grass and entertain the ladies and their children.

Frances brought her oil paints outside and completed several small pictures but said she was not satisfied with any of them. "They are just too small for the majesty of this huge country," she complained to Bette.

Having grown up watching a house full of Beechey artists, Bette did not contradict her sister. Instead she said, "You could just make the paintings larger, Frances." That only brought on a tirade of how small the house was with no place for any type of studio. "Well, then," Bette's voice was placating, "you could just keep a journal like the other company wives do. Then you wouldn't need a studio." It was exactly the wrong thing to suggest.

"You don't understand at all, do you Bette? I don't want to *write* about my experience here. That would be so dull, so—colorless. I have a talent, thanks to our father and Grandpapa Beechey. While I am here, I want to draw and paint. I want my pictures to speak for me. To *show*, not tell, the hugeness of life here. Now do you understand?"

All Bette could understand was that along with producing babies, Frances was beginning to be very serious about producing quality artistic creations.

It was Della who brought news that put an abrupt end to their idyllic summer. She ran full speed through the open kitchen doors and said breathlessly to Nell, "Gramma! Mr. Hopkins is back already! Governor Simpson is very ill!"

"There's not much to wonder about, Nell," Old Maud McGuire said as they sat on a sunny bench just off Front Street. "That little man is completely done in."

"Then what will happen with the royal visit and all?" Nell asked.

"That is the only item keeping himself in his bed. The doctor has told the governor that he would be dead before the prince arrives, otherwise. So here sits me gossipin' when I've come across to shop for all the good soup bones one can stuff into a pot. I'm to do all in my power to restore him before the end of August. Any suggestions?"

The governor was "restored" in time to act the perfect host, or so it seemed to those who did not know him better. Frances and Bette stood for their party gown fittings and had to endure the teasing of Nora and Millie, who said that Frances was taking on every pound that Bette was losing. Spirits rose with the governor's improving health and the approaching festivities.

Della thought Albert Edward, Prince of Wales, was deliciously handsome. Of course she had had a mere glimpse of him boarding his barge when the Royal Party had shoved off into the river. The prince, who could be recognized only by his youth amid so many old admirals, dukes, earls, and such, wore bright red military dress and looked, indeed, princely. While in her final class at Saint Anne's that spring, Della had been engaged in quite a study of the Royal Family. Albert Edward was Queen Victoria's eldest son and would one day be king. He would be visiting Ottawa to lay the cornerstone for the long-awaited parliament buildings, and along the way he would stop in Lachine as the guest of the Hudson's Bay Company and Sir George Simpson, Governor.

It was on his outward crossing to the formal reception on Isle Dorval that Della, Millie, and Nora had seen the prince. After days of hectic planning, preparations, and parties at Hopkins House, the young ladies had been given this day free, as the boys would be looked after by the governesses of friends their own ages. Their parents would be at Governor Simpson's luncheon for the prince and the other dignitaries.

"I don't envy Mrs. Hopkins having to spend the whole afternoon with all those old men," Della said to her companions.

"What about Mr. Hopkins?" retorted Millie. "He is old, but he is also very pleasant."

Nora laughed at the girls' innocence. "Don't worry," she told them, "Madame is sure to find one among the whiskered, limping old gentlemen to talk with about those paintings she so loves to view."

Not only did Frances talk about paintings that day, she actually began to make one. For her, making a sketch was the beginning of painting a picture. Bette frowned and poked her elbow into Frances but Edward only smiled, seeing that his wife had taken her little sketchbook from her reticule and within moments, had drawn an amazingly detailed sketch of the canoes that were waiting to join the prince's barge mid-river.

Three days later Della had just finished reading an account of the royal visit in Mr. Hopkins' discarded *Montreal Gazette* when Millie used Miss Nora's best fabric scissors to cut out the article. Millie said, "I want to include this in a letter I am sending to my parents back in England. You don't mind, do you, Della? The clipping will spare me so much writing."

"I can't remember everything the article said, Gramma Nell," Della said later. "But I know that Mrs. Hopkins and Miss Beechey and one other were the only ladies invited to the luncheon with the prince. Isn't that wonderful!"

"What I want to know about is the People's part in it," Nell said. "I heard that the young prince was given a ride back here to Lachine in your father's canoe. Is that true? And if so, why hasn't Big Louie been in here bragging all over us about that honor?"

Della had had similar thoughts, which she had kept to herself. But then, Papa always had to be where the governor wanted him to be, not elsewhere.

"All right, Gramma. I'll try to get the happenings in order," she continued.

"The prince and all the dignified gentlemen started to the island in their military boats. But when they got to the middle of the St.

Lawrence, Papa's and eight other canoes were there to meet him. All nine canoes were so beautiful! They had flags bow and stern and every man in them was dressed like an Indian whether he really was one or not. Most of the men were from Caughnawaga, but the paper said that some men had come from Lake of Two Mountains. The reporter said that they all wore feathers and scarlet cloth and even war paint. Do you think that was true, Gramma?"

"What I think doesn't matter, since I don't know. But I think that if the governor told Louie to have the men do that, then that is exactly what they all did."

Della smiled. "Shouldn't we be getting dinner while we talk?" she asked suddenly, realizing that they had been sitting over their tea for quite some time.

"Not yet," Gramma answered. "The family hasn't come home yet, so I'm just holding off on everything. Go on with your telling, child."

"Hmm. Where was I?"

"Out in the middle of the St. Lawrence surrounded by a hundred wild Indians and one teenage prince," laughed her grandmother.

"Yes. So when the prince's barge got to the canoes, all at once the canoes swung around and made a straight line on each side of the barge and our men sang the prince all the way to Isle Dorval. Then they cheered when he landed, and—listen to this, Gramma—the prince was so happy that he saluted the voyageurs! That means that Papa received a salute from the prince!" She wondered again when Papa might come to tell her more about the event.

Nell pushed herself up from the table and went through to the street side to see if her people were coming yet. Della continued, "I don't think Mrs. Hopkins will say anything to us about the party in Governor Simpson's island house. She is not one to talk like that, but maybe you will hear something from Old Maud."

Gramma had returned, shaking her graying head, and put more wood into the cook stove. "You better finish up, sweet one. I think there may finally be movement down the road apiece."

"Well, then. The paper said that a military band played some music outside. Then it was time for everybody to come back across. So the prince and a general and a duke, or somebody, got into Papa's canoe—well, the paper didn't say that, but it said the *front* canoe—and they all came back because…Now, Gramma, this is what the reporter said happened—because Governor Simpson was in the middle of the canoe brigade himself and he was telling them all what to do!"

When Mr. and Mrs. Hopkins finally did come home they didn't want any dinner. Word came to the kitchen by way of Millie that Governor Simpson had had an attack of apoplexy—a stroke! It was all Nell could do to keep from saying out loud, "Serves the old fool right, not taking care of himself."

She regretted even that unspoken thought a few days later when news came that Sir George Simpson, twenty-one-year governor-in-chief of Rupert's Land, the huge area owned by the Hudson's Bay Company in North America (and dearest friend to Edward Hopkins), was dead.

VII

Changes

"I just can't believe it!" Millie said. "How could she do it? And on the very day that the governor died, too?"

"But Millie," Della pointed out, and not for the first time, "Miss Nora could not have known that the governor would die on *that* day. Not that she would have altered her plans if she had known, but, well…"

This was the second week and the topic of kitchen conversation had not changed: the death of Governor Simpson and the elopement of Mademoiselle Lenore LaFleur. Both subjects had been chewed and analyzed to the point of exhaustion. At last, Nell Gunn presented a new subject. She said to her young charges, "I'm not wanting to upset you young ones even further, but, as you might be expecting—if you could tear yourselves away from Miss Nora's desertion for a moment—our family needs be making plans to move into their own future." The girls understood when Nell used "our family" that she meant the Hopkins family. They sat in silence, realizing for the first time that their lives, too, would continue to move along, just not with the same cast of characters that had recently inhabited them.

"What do you mean, Gramma—'move into their own future'?" Della asked.

"Exactly that, Della. I should think that you are old enough to realize nothing remains the same. Who do you think will run the company? How will Mr. Hopkins spend his time now that the old governor is gone? And of less importance, but nearly as distressing to poor Mrs. Hopkins, who will outfit this growing family now that that little French…" Nell stopped mid-sentence before harsh words regarding Miss Nora slipped out.

The girls looked sheepishly at their hands. Both felt guilty about their lack of mature comprehension of the situation. Then, as she had for the past six years, Della counted on her grandmother's guidance. "What do you think will happen now, Gramma?" Millie also looked with anxiety at the old woman.

"There will be changes, of course, and you will be part of them," Nell finally said.

Except for the kitchen, the house had been quiet since Governor Simpson's funeral in Montreal. Naturally, Mr. and Mrs. Hopkins had attended, as had every person of standing in the region. Della and Millie could only speculate on actual events, but surely Colin Fraser, the governor's personal piper, had taken part. The girls knew the musician by sight and were acquainted with several of his numerous children.

Mr. Steven had again shown his worth during the period of mourning. He had encouraged the boys to focus on Colin Fraser's attachment to his employer, Sir George Simpson. The tutor reminded the boys that, just as Big Louie had been at the governor's call, so had been his piper, Mr. Fraser. When the boys, understanding the seriousness of the situation and their father's grief (yet still being young boys), wanted a story that wouldn't be sad, Mr. Steven had found one.

"Ogden," he had begun. "Do you think that Mr. Fraser's bagpipe looks like a swan?" The second brother laughed delightedly.

"Manley, do you think Mr. Fraser's hairy legs and skirt make him look like a woman?"

"No-o-o." The boys laughed in unison.

"Weel, naugh," continued their teacher, putting the brogue on extra thick, "once when your papa and Governor Simpson were away up at Norway House, that company post out west by Lake Winnipeg, this Cree Indian fella saw and heard Mr. Fraser play his bagpipes and reported back to his chief, saying something like this: "One white man was dressed like a woman in a skirt of a funny color. He had whiskers growing from his belt and fancy leggings."

The boys began laughing again and punched at each other. Mr. Steven waited a moment before continuing: "This lady-man carried a black swan which had many legs with ribbons tied to them. The swan's body was upside down under his arm and he put its head in his mouth and bit it."

Going through the motions brought another outburst from the boys, which made Mr. Steven glad that the parents were away, even if it was to attend a funeral. The teacher continued: "At the same time that he was biting, the lady-man pinched the swan's neck with his fingers and squeezed its body with his arm. That is why such terrible noise came out of the animal."

In their lightened spirits, the boys could not know that this would be among the last of their lessons with Mr. Colin Steven. The changes Gramma Nell had predicted were just beginning.

* * *

Della hurried up the attic steps to the little room that Millie now had to herself. Dinner was about to be served, and Mrs. Hopkins had asked to speak to the girls together.

"What is it, Della? Are we retiring? Going back home?" Millie asked.

They learned of their future only moments later while sitting with Mrs. Hopkins in the side parlor.

"My dears," Mrs. Hopkins began, "I have news for you both." They could only wait impatiently. "First," Frances announced, "you may have guessed that we have another baby on the way." Della certainly had not "guessed," but Millie didn't seem surprised. "And fortunately, with that event, the next news is not unwelcome: we will be moving into a larger house in Montreal where Mr. Hopkins has already taken over duties of the Lachine establishment."

Millie gave a little clap and hugged Della, who was much more subdued. Frances seemed to understand their very different reactions to her announcements. She said to Millie, "Cousin, why don't you tell Mrs. Gunn that we will be in shortly."

Privately, Frances said to Della, "Your grandmother prefers to stay with this house, as she always has done, but wants you to make your own decision about staying or coming with us, Della. I assure you that you are wanted and needed, now that—well, now that we have been left with a sewing machine and no one else to operate it. In addition, I would so much miss your company."

Della was momentarily stunned. Gramma! Papa!

"You don't have to decide right now, Della. Come. Let us not keep Mrs. Gunn waiting."

VIII

Growing Pains

The most noticeable changes that first year in Montreal were in Frances Anne Hopkins. Della mentioned them in a letter dated June 1861:

Dear Gramma Nell,

I don't know how she does it! I am so in awe of Mrs. Hopkins. She has become three women in one! First, of course, she is the wife and hostess for all of Mr. Hopkins' important company and political friends. Then, she is mother to five very active boys, two of them still mere babies. And most exciting, she is an artist!

Remember those little drawings Mrs. H. used to put into that book her mother had given her? Well, Gramma, she has used some of those sketches to create larger, wonderfully beautiful paintings!

Now, I know this is what you will be most interested in learning. I am well and happy. Sharing a room with Millie is delightful, and I preferred that by far to sharing with one of the new housemaids. Millie and I don't do much of that type of work anymore. We both seem to have more defined roles here than we did in Lachine. That is because life here seems to move so much faster.

Millie spends most of her time with baby Wilfred or playing with Raymond who, after learning to walk, would be into every-thing if Millie weren't constantly on his track. As with the older boys, the babies adore Millie.

I am afraid I have not been as useful to Mrs. Hopkins as Nora was, but I'm learning. At first I sewed muslin undergarments for us all. That was a good way to learn to make the machine (and me!) go faster without having all my mistakes on display. Some items we can buy ready-made in the new Ladies' Department of the company store, or even in one of the other shops in the Center. As Mrs. H. sometimes wishes to have me accompany her when she goes out, I have taken a pattern from the nicest of the dresses which Nora made for Millie and re-worked it into a new dress for myself. You won't be surprised when I tell you that this fine dress (under which I must now use a wider hoop!) is a soft blue. The over-jacket is a darker blue silk with many, many yards of ruffled fabric. My talent, Mrs. H. says, is in bonnet making. But, of course, anyone could do well with a little frame and a good deal of lace.

I'm sorry I've spent so much of my writing time on fashions, Gramma. Now I'll tell what we do in them. Of course Millie and I are very much in the background, but we never doubt that our services are valued. "How could I be as active as I am without my two dears?" Mrs. H. asks when her lady friends quiz her. Not that all the other fine ladies don't also have their "fine dears."

But Millie and I have allowed ourselves to feel very special in the operation of this busy household. However, Gramma Dear, that doesn't mean that I'm not thinking of you and the others at Lachine every day. Please give each of them a smile from

Your loving granddaughter,
Della Isobel Macleod

It was Wednesday afternoon again and Della and Millie were walking up Côte des Neiges and away from Hopkins House, a handsome two-storied structure topped with various chimneys, turrets, and gables. First they would stop by the Postal Receiving Office, then meet friends on Mount Royal.

"I don't understand why we can't have pillar boxes for our letters here in Montreal as they do in Toronto," complained Millie. "And why did they have to change the rules and make *me* pay for the stamp here on this side of the ocean? My parents were always happy to pay on the British side. But that's because I'm not as faithful about writing to them as you are to your Gramma Nell."

Each girl carried a stamped letter, but only Millie felt self-satisfied in having nearly completed a dreary chore.

"I say, Millie. You're surely not going to ruin our afternoon out by complaining about a task already finished, are you?" Della scolded.

Just as Millie was about to answer, Della stopped short in her tracks. "Oh, how silly of me! I wrote in this letter that I would tell Gramma what we do when we go out together on our free afternoon. Then I didn't even tell her!"

They laughed together as they had years earlier when first they had become friends. "Well, next time you write that dear old lady you can say that we climbed up Royal Mountain to visit the resting place of someone she admired: Governor George Simpson of the glorious HBC." Millie playfully patted the cheeks of her younger friend until they were nearly as rosy as her own.

There were four figures waiting near the grave marker of Governor Simpson and his wife instead of just the two they had expected. The young ladies were sisters, Elizabeth and Abigail Ross. Both worked in the household of the governor of Rupert's Land. The gentlemen, however, were unfamiliar to Della and Millie. The girls advanced more slowly, wondering if a larger party would alter the afternoon they had planned with the Ross sisters.

Mr. Robert Eaton was an Irish emigrant in search of just the right business into which he and his brothers could devote their many talents. He was tall, whiskered, and overly confident of his abilities (the girls agreed later). Mr. Alan Scott was another matter. First officer on the HBC steamer *Labouchere*, he was spending shore time visiting his cousins Betsy and Abby Ross. Mr. Scott hung back a bit and appeared to be as unsure of himself as the other gentleman was the opposite.

The most convenient topic for the group to take up was Mr. and Mrs. Simpson, who reposed immediately before them. While Mr. Scott knew much about the one-time company governor, Mr. Eaton invited some local history from the ladies who had lived so near the renowned man. Before Millie could offer the scandalous information she knew, Della began a little recital, walking slowly around the tombstones, then on down the tree-lined pathway. This left Mr. Scott and the three other ladies to drift along in her wake. And it left Miss Millie in deep waters before the afternoon was over.

That night in their attic room the girls talked endlessly of the day's encounter. Millie was sure she was in love, but said, "And what good would that do even if Mr. Scott had eyes for me? How often am I likely to see a man of the sea?" They both laughed at her little word game.

"Millie," Della soothed. "You never know what fate has in store for you. Why, maybe someday you'll sail back home to England right on *Captain* Scott's own ship. You have lots of years left before anyone could call you an old maid."

It wasn't someone, but some*thing* from Hopkins House that made the return voyage to Britain with Mr. Scott and the *Labouchere*. One of Frances Anne's pictures, the first of many to be exhibited by her in London, was stowed on board.

Frances herself was not feeling well. Though generally exceptionally healthy, she now became tired and pale. By autumn she was sure she was pregnant again. However, this time the experience was not to be a pleasant one, and the child to come was not a robust little boy, as Raymond and Wilfred had been.

Millie did everything possible to assist her cousin during the pregnancy and after the delivery, but Frances refused to be idle. The infant was sickly and occupied more time and attention than Millie had to give, as she gave so much to his two next-older brothers, not much more than babies themselves.

It was decided then, that Della and the new baby would remain in Montreal with the nurse while the family made a trip back to England. Frances' sister, Katherine, had been widowed early in 1862, and the lively Hopkins family visit was much anticipated to ease her mourning.

The wet nurse, called Mrs. Flynn, had had some medical training before her marriage and came highly recommended by Dr. Decker. The woman agreed to live in while the family was abroad and Dr. Decker agreed to call in every week, whether needed by little William or not. It was to be a summer of learning for teen-aged Della, for Mrs. Flynn liked to talk as she nursed the baby.

"This babe's not long for the world, would be my impression," Mrs. Flynn said one sunny morning.

Della was shocked. "Why, Mrs. Flynn, how can you say such a thing? Baby seems to be a little stronger every day. And he certainly knows who I am when I sing to or play with him."

Mrs. Flynn did not give in easily. "The missus has had too many too fast," the nurse said.

Della remained thoughtful. It was true enough that Mrs. Hopkins had been "indisposed" nearly half the time since she had come to Canada. Della felt it improper to continue this discussion, yet knew that more appropriate opportunities seldom were presented. She felt that she needed to know about such things.

"The nuns at my school said that God sends babies to their mother. Then, Mrs. Flynn, how can there be too many babies if each one is sent by God?"

The older woman gently moved Baby Hopkins to her other bulging breast. Before she had married and begun her own family, she also thought that God gave babies. With some secret reading and lots of conversation with women of her own social class, she now knew that a woman might, if she chose, somewhat influence the number of God's gifts. But what right did she have to speak of such things to this girl?

"Have you not discussed this with your own mother, Missy Della?"

Knowing that an answer was expected, Della whispered, "I have only a grandmother."

"Well, then. At your age, it's best someone speaks up." Mrs. Flynn paused. "Your women—on the other side of the river—have always had, well, shall we say—methods. Usually this means not being with their man for a period of time." She gave a sniffing laugh. "That, however, is made decidedly easier when that man has other wives or other women to be with. You *do* know about being with a man, don't you, Della?" The girl blushed, but nodded her head.

"Then—there are things the men can do, also." Della had never considered this. In her young mind, babies came from their mothers.

At this point, cook called from below that, if they were hungry, they must come down at once or miss out. Consequently, Della had to give up one type of hunger to satisfy another.

It was the following summer before Della had opportunity to continue the topic she had once discussed with Mrs. Flynn. She was at home when Gramma Nell asked about the wee babe, as she called him. "No, he hasn't learned to walk yet, but he keeps trying." Della took a deep breath. "Gramma, is it true that having babies can wear out their mother's body?"

Nell had never been one to jump into an answer. As she often did, she countered with a question of her own. "Are you worried about our Mrs. Hopkins, then, sweet one?"

Della nodded. "Oh, Gramma. She is such a busy lady. Every visitor to Montreal seems to end up at our house. Mrs. H. keeps my fingers flying in wardrobe preparation. Why, you would think that the gowns she brought from London would be enough, but there are always new items for the children to be stitched. And—oh, Gramma!—she's looking so white again. I'm afraid—yes, actually afraid that, well… I can say this to you Gramma. I'm afraid there might be another baby on the way."

Nell was silent, then patted the girl's moist hand. "Such is life, my sweet, when folks care for each other as our Mr. and Mrs. Hopkins do."

IX

All at Sea

Later that summer Millie, along with the entire Hopkins family, made an Atlantic crossing. The time had arrived for the older boys to be placed in school. While Gouverneur and Ogden were being settled in Sussex, and Frances had the assistance of her sisters with the two babies, Millie could travel farther west to be reunited with her own country family. It was a plan to be successfully repeated numerous times in the coming years. The difficult part was keeping children occupied during the Atlantic crossings.

The older boys could pretty well look after themselves, and little Manley was never far from his beloved mamma. With one babe still in arms, that really left only young Raymond to be closely attended. Frances was able to work a bit on ideas for future paintings and Edward was never at a loss for company paperwork. His status with the company ensured comfortable quarters, if not spacious accommodation aboard the steamship. The crossing of less than two weeks' time became nearly a private vacation for the entire family.

Miss Millie Stapleton was not aware that she made a striking picture as governess to Mr. Hopkins' dear little boys. In her forest green traveling costume, with a child at one hand and a book in the other, only the curls of flaming red hair that could not be captured under the bonnet Della had fashioned gave hint that she was not as

54

fine a lady as her cousin, Mrs. Edward Hopkins.

Millie may, indeed, have turned some heads, but the only man who interested her on board (since Mr. Alan Scott was *not*) was an old carpenter called Davieo. He may have been Spanish or Italian and his real name surely wasn't what he was called, but she and one or more of the boys sat listening to his stories nearly every afternoon.

Mr. Davieo had a tabby cat called Senora Wallis. (The cat was called this name on their first meeting at least. When they met the pair in future times, it was either a different cat or was called by a different name.) Mr. Davieo and Senora Cat had a little cubby near the ship's stern, and if the boys went missing, Millie knew where to look first for them.

On this first crossing it was not the cat, but monkeys that held the boys' interest. It was the middle brother, Ogden, who had found Mr. Davieo sitting in the sun carving a small block of wood.

"May I ask, sir, what it is you are making?" Ogden said timidly.

The young lad in his fine clothes was not the first to have taken an interest in Davieo's pastime. "It will be monkeys before we reach the other side," the old man answered.

"How many monkeys from that small block?" Ogden asked.

"Hmm…" Davieo stalled, allowing the boy more time to watch the flying wood chips.

No answer was forthcoming, so Ogden continued, "Why monkeys, if I may ask, sir."

"Because they are wise," came the carver's answer.

The following afternoon Ogden returned to the stern, leading his two brothers and Miss Millie. "This is Mr. Davieo," he said proudly. "He is carving monkeys."

"*See no evil! Hear no evil! Speak no evil!*" Davieo said, pointing his carving knife at each boy in turn.

Millie had to conceal a smile as the boys' eyes became more and more round. She stepped back to watch them enjoy the experience.

"You see, young gentlemen," the carver began, "a long, long time ago, I rode the sailing ships to Japan—away across the other side of the world." His hands worked steadily as he spoke. "Not so very many like me have visited such places, but there is much to be learned there.

"Do you know the Nikko Toshogu shrine there?" Each boy swung his head from side to side. "Well, young sirs, there is one. And carved above the entrance to that shrine are the first wise monkeys. Are you sure you haven't seen them?" Again the slowly moving young heads.

"The stories say that the idea for these three wise monkeys comes from—oh—from someplace else in the Far East, like India or China maybe. But the idea stays the same: number one monkey—this will be him, here on the right—he *sees* nothing bad. Number two, on the left, he *hears* nothing bad. And that leaves monkey number three, to be placed between his brothers to *say* nothing bad. Well, I do declare! That would be just like you three, wouldn't it?"

"But we have two more little brothers with us," said Manley. "What about them?"

"Ah! That is not a problem at all. For all the other little monkeys—and little boys of the world—there is the most important thing."

"But, sir," said Ogden. "What *is* the most important thing?"

"Why, sonny. That would be to *do* no evil!" Davieo ended with a tremendous laughing roar, leading Millie to conclude that only in the latter years of his life had the carver adhered to the fourth monkey's idea.

As promised, just prior to landing on English shores, the carving of the three little monkeys was finished. Davieo gave it to Ogden, promising on some future voyage to do others for his brothers. The old man pointed to the right hand figure, whose hands covered his eyes and the boys said, "*See no evil!*" To the left where the monkey's teeth showed but his ears were covered, they said, "*Hear no evil!*" And lastly to the center where all repeated, "*Speak no evil!*"

"And which of you fellas will grow up to be a carver like old

Davieo?" the man asked.

It was Ogden who answered, saying, "I think maybe if we are to be artists, Mr. Davieo, we will need to be painters. You see, our mamma is a very good painter and she gets to show her pictures at the best art houses in the city of London."

Davieo frowned a little and looked to Millie for confirmation. Millie just smiled and nodded her head slowly up and down.

After Governor Simpson's death, Edward Hopkins had been promoted to more high-level administrative responsibility with the company. He was now chief factor in charge of the affairs of the Montreal Department of the HBC. As he no longer was required to travel as extensively on tours of inspection, he had more time to spend with his family. He and Frances spent some of the quiet hours aboard ship discussing their future. Edward appreciated his wife's artistic talent. He was, in fact, very proud of her work and of her interest in the outdoor subjects that had occupied his life for more than twenty years.

"My dear Frances," Edward said during one trip that was (as they all became) part company business and part personal business, "one day in the not-so-distant future, I would like to give up this hectic life and retire to a home in the English countryside. It would have a large, quiet, and sunny studio where you could paint and I could sit and read and watch."

"That sounds wonderful, indeed, Edward. However, I would need to have—well, something interesting and challenging *to* paint."

They sat quietly and were soothed by the movement of the ship. Then Edward asked in his kindly and supportive fashion, "What is the subject, my dear, that would most interest you?" He did not doubt that she would have a ready answer. And she did, but she came to it in her own way.

"If you think it could be arranged, Edward, I would like to travel more often with you. By canoe. I told sister Bette once that my 'Canadian Journal' would be my pictures, and yet, to this point, the most exciting of those scenes has not been put to canvas."

"On a guess, that would be the brigade of canoes which welcomed the Prince of Wales?"

"Oh, Edward. You begin to know me too well!" She hid her blushing face behind dainty little hands.

"Is it the Canadian scenery you wish for subject, then Frances? Or, are you thinking more in terms of the Canadian way of life—the canoe life—which is fading more and more completely with every new steamship and railway line?"

"That would be the challenge, Edward. To paint both at the same time." She paused and smoothed some hair strands back into their net. "At present, there is little interest on either side of this ocean for pictures of—well, of canoes and the men who move them. But...even if I only paint those scenes as a record for our own children, Edward, that in itself would be worth the while. The boys will have their lives on the British side of the Atlantic someday, but I would never want them to forget the land of their birth."

Throughout that autumn and the very cold Canadian winter, an extension off the Hopkins' Côte de Neiges kitchen was turned into a working studio—not a large one like Frances would eventually have in her English houses, but the first private, professional space she had had since her marriage. Frances had the walls papered with a narrow neutral vertical stripe, so as to make the space appear larger. She had Della use a heavy, cream-colored lace for curtains that could be pulled to block the sun coming across the garden at some seasons, but not the light that was always necessary for accurate depiction of color. The career of FAH, as she would sign her pictures, had begun.

X

White Water

Her life now had a personal direction, apart from husband and children, but it wasn't as though Frances Anne Hopkins had to plan situations that led to future works of art. To Della it seemed that Mrs. Hopkins' mind itself was a canvas on which she stored minute details of everyday or of special-day life.

Montreal of the early 1860s was a city of much excitement. So many events were happening daily that newspapers could hardly keep up. As she worked Mrs. Hopkins often asked Della to read from the headlines or through articles of interest, so that Della, too, kept abreast of the latest in political, scientific, medical, and literary affairs. But when those topics became too heavy or depressing, Frances would request a reading from her favorite poet, Henry W. Longfellow, the American.

"I'm sorry, Mrs. Hopkins," Della said one day after reading an article concerning the Civil War, raging in its third year in the southeastern part of the United States. "I don't understand why we in Canada, who have not allowed slavery since—oh, so many years—are still a little more sympathetic toward the Confederate States. What is it that I am not aware of?"

Frances was hugely pregnant again and sitting feet up with her sketchbook open. She felt too tired at the moment to offer more than a brief explanation. "There are some in this area," she said, "who would not be displeased to have a smaller, weaker neighbor to the immediate south."

An invention that had first come on the scene shortly before the American Civil War saw some refinement during that conflict. Shortly after the birth of Olive Beechey Hopkins, the photographic camera recorded for posterity the face of her mother, the artist.

"Della," Frances said, after passing her squirming infant daughter to a delighted Cousin Millie, "you and I are going off to make another little surprise for Mr. Hopkins."

Della had never known quite how to behave when the usually serious Mrs. Hopkins became playful. To be safe she generally smiled and moved in whatever direction was indicated. This time she fetched her next-best shawl and bonnet and followed out the side door.

Their destination was the studio of a man called Mr. Notman, who was making some progress in business as a portrait photographer.

"Do you think me a traitor, Della?" asked Frances.

Because she did not know what possibility there could be of that—surely nothing to do with the Civil War in the South!—Della answered, "Of course not, Mrs. Hopkins, though to be honest—I'm sorry—I don't know what you mean by the question."

"You are the sweetest among all young ladies in Montreal, Della Macleod. Honestly, I believe you are. Do you not see the irony in a painter, and the granddaughter of a well-known painter of royal faces, having her picture made by—well, by a machine?"

"Oh, you mean Mr. Notman's camera, then." Della had to smile to herself. Months ago she (and some of the other servants too, probably) had overheard a lively discussion—yes, that was the civilized term for it—between Mr. and Mrs. Hopkins about her having what he had called her "picture *taken*." Mrs. Hopkins was resisting, offering various excuses, chief among them that it might be possible to tell that, as she put it, she was "not alone" in the picture. Mr. Hopkins disagreed, but relented, as long as his wife promised to go to Mr. Notman as soon after the birth as she thought proper. That was their errand at present.

Della thought that her employer was dressed too severely for what might be a fun outing. Her dark wool gown had abalone shell buttons marching down the front. The white lace collar and cuffs softened the effect a little, but it was the small, round brooch that gave the attractive twenty-five-year-old the look of a matron.

Mr. Notman had become adept at placing his customers at their ease. Della helped Frances arrange herself on the portrait chair, and then, just before turning away, wet her finger and tucked a few strands of the lady's hair back over her right ear. She was about to ask if she might pinch some color up into the pale cheeks when she remembered that the magic camera-box would not notice color anyway. The girl stepped back out of range and smiled at the neutral look Mrs. Hopkins managed to hold for the required length of time. That, Della thought, was that. Quick and easy. A process that would be the death of generations of oil painters, such as the famous Sir William Beechey.

Of course she should have known. Nothing was that easy. After the close-up portrait-picture of Mrs. Hopkins came several others, and each required an entire costume change. "Ah! So that's why I am along," the girl thought. "Dressing maid!"

But the longer they were in the studio, the more fun the process became.

Mr. William Notman was a Scot of about the same age as Mr. Hopkins. Immigrating to Canada a year or two before Frances had come over, he was already well known in Montreal's elite circles as the best portrait photographer. But, because he was also a practical Scot, he always encouraged his patrons to try some additional popular poses of the day, not just one formal sitting.

While still in her formal black dress, Mr. Notman had Frances pose as a grand lady about to receive visitors. Della draped a fine black lace shawl around her "mistress" and attached a velvet ribbon over her head to secure a matching lace mantilla. Frances placed her right hand on a delicately carved wooden table and the whole effect was perfect for the 1860s formal portrait.

Next was a character from Shakespeare whom Della had never seen on stage, though she vaguely remembered her as inhabiting *The Merchant of Venice*. Portia represented the qualities of the perfect wife. And though Della did not care at all for this picture, so dark and judgmental, Frances certainly possessed Portia's qualities.

The last full-length picture was, or could have been, the best; however, Della thought they would never get the shepherdess costume arranged well enough to suit Mr. Notman. First, Frances had to change her hose from black to white. Then they attached big white bows to her own black shoes. The skirt was a very dark pink with an overskirt and bodice of bright flowers on a white background. Atop Mrs. Hopkins' hair, which was still enclosed in a black net, Della placed a white house cap. On each wrist was a black velvet band and a similar band was wrapped around her neck. Oh! The effect was marvelous! Then, just before the picture was to be taken, Frances decided to add a long, white, gauzy apron. She stuffed her hands into the apron's pockets and smiled like a girl.

"Oh, Mrs. Hopkins, you look absolutely wonderful!" Della said. Why don't you smile for this picture? It would not be inappropriate to the setting." But Mr. Notman explained that, though less formal than the other poses, even a slight smile would be difficult to hold for the time needed to expose the photograph.

When at last the photographic session was completed, the ladies still did not exit the shop immediately because Frances had questions.

"Might I inquire, Mr. Notman, do you make all of your pictures here in your studio?"

Mrs. Edward (Frances Anne) Hopkins as a shepherdess, Montreal, QC, 1863.
Notman Photographic Archives, McCord Museum, Montreal.

The photographer seemed pleased by her interest. "Why, yes, madam. I do." He noticed her look of disappointment. "Why do you ask?"

"I have seen photographic images of battle scenes to the south. I had supposed that pictures—say of the countryside—could be made here in Canada, too."

"Indeed they could be, good lady. And at one time, before I came inside, so to speak, I carried these heavy instruments here and there to do exactly that. Would you have any interest in viewing some of my outdoor work?"

Della saw her companion nearly leap with interest. That faded, however, with the appearance of each successive photograph. One after another gray and white scene was laid aside without comment by Frances.

"Do you believe, Mr. Notman, that the day will ever come when the photographs will have color to them?"

"Yes, of course. Tomorrow, for example. I could have my assistant add color to your own face and hands. Excuse me, Mrs. Hopkins. I meant, of course, to those parts which will be shown in the portraits we only now have completed."

As the ladies were making their way home, Della said what Frances had been silently thinking. "If the color has to be added later anyway, why not just paint the picture to begin with?"

"There is that," Frances said slowly. "But...think of the photograph in another way, Della. Think of it as the sketch which could lay the foundation for a painting. Later in the artistic process, questions regarding placement, proportion, detail, and so on would be eliminated. Yes. Yes, I can envision this new instrument not as a competitor, but—well, as a tool. As an artist's assistant!" It was seldom that Mrs. Hopkins allowed herself to become so animated.

Within a year's time Frances was wishing that she had Mr. Notman's camera along to make "sketches" for her. Then, later, she was glad that she did not have the extra baggage. Edward, as promised, had invited her along on his 1864 inspection tour as far west as Fort William.

They had traveled outward via American steamship along the south shore of Lake Superior and with company business completed, planned to return home by way of the old canoe routes. However, as they neared the Sault Ste. Marie area, Edward became ill. The thought of camping in the middle of the wilderness with only their voyageurs as medical attendants did not appeal at all to Mrs. Hopkins. Though Frances herself was hale and hearty, she and her husband returned to Lachine by steamer and rail.

Frances found that there were some situations that could only be captured in memory. Two of these occurred in the company of the new governor of Rupert's Land, Mr. Alexander Grant Dallas, successor to old Governor Simpson.

George Simpson had named Alexander Dallas to take over the governorship shortly before he died. Mr. Dallas had not had a long history with the company, but had been notably successful in assignments in regions west of the Rocky Mountains. With the discovery of gold in British Columbia came many of the same people and problems that had plagued California under similar conditions a decade earlier. Old Mr. Douglas, the company's chief factor of the western region, had more than his hands full with an influx of miners into his fur trading region. And he had a beautiful daughter, too. Mr. Dallas had not made a friend of the chief factor, but he had made a wife of the factor's daughter.

Like so many of the company women, Jane Douglas was a daughter "of the country," meaning the girl had ancestors among the First People of Canada. But Mr. Dallas cared not about her background or about his disagreements with her father concerning company business. He married Jane Douglas and before long brought her east, through Montreal.

Naturally, when Governor Dallas and his wife arrived in Montreal, they were entertained by Edward and Frances. The Hopkinses, along with Mr. Watkins of the International Financial Society, a company that had taken controlling interest in the HBC, accompanied Governor Dallas in his canoe on sightseeing tours. Then, for sheer excitement, they took his canoe through the Lachine rapids back to Montreal.

As the four still-excited passengers were having a celebratory dinner after their rapids-shooting excitement, Della sat with Millie in the upstairs nursery. Tiny baby Olive slept peacefully in Millie's arms, but their rocking chair moved in agitation.

"Oh, I get so irritated!" Millie was saying. "I'm just glad I knew nothing of that escapade until it was safely over!"

"Now, Millie. Don't get so worked up. You'll disturb the baby." Della patted the older girl on the arm and peered at little Olive.

"I know, I know. It's quite a thrill for the English visitors to ride a canoe through the white water. But I believe it to be quite unnecessary to risk the lives of *both* of this baby's parents to do it." Millie tightened her mouth in an ugly scowl.

"Millie. Shame on you. Do you really think that sixteen strong voyageurs would allow any disaster to fall upon such important passengers?"

"No. No, of course they wouldn't—willingly. But my heart is always with these little children and the ones away from us. And I just don't know what I would do if anything bad happened."

Della could see now that her friend was truly upset. She talked on quietly. "It's just that people like Mr. Watkins must be sent back to London with the best of memories of their time here in Canada. They must have—umm—I think we could call them—yes, 'novel stories' to tell their business associates and the members of their fancy London clubs."

"Yes, but what of a nice lady like Cousin Frances. Why does *she* need to do such dangerous things? Especially when she has all these little ones to mother?"

Having grown up with such "dangerous things" a part of everyday life, Della did not point out that rapids running was quite a normal activity to people like her father. She said instead, "I suppose someday Mrs. Hopkins will make a painting of today's canoe adventure and it will hang in a fine room as *her* memory of Canada."

XI

Hearing Voices

It was the impression of *movement* of the long Montreal canoe through the Lachine rapids that Frances knew Mr. Notman's camera could never picture. Why, she had not even been allowed to blink her eyes when he had made her portraits! A second image the mechanical camera could never duplicate, she had already achieved: she had painted a campfire burning in the dark. In fact, she had done two fires in the same picture: a torch glowing in plain sight and a campfire partially hidden behind a voyageur. Though she had been pleased and excited by the result of her fires, she felt that she had somewhat misused her time and effort.

In her excitement to try the new glowing flame techniques, she had painted over an old canvas that happened to be of the large size she desired. The original picture (now lying under that of some voyageurs repairing an upturned canoe by firelight) had been of a riverside house and its overgrown gardens. "I do not find this scene *picturesque*," she told Della. She had not even bothered to prepare the canvas surface anew, but simply painted over the old picture.

Since Olive's birth Frances sometimes felt that time was moving too fast. She often missed the older children more than she had thought possible. Manley was away in Sussex with his brothers, and Raymond and Wilfred could hardly be considered babies now that

William and Olive had arrived.

She had kept an especially close eye on Edward after his illness, but he appeared to have regained his vigor completely. Baby Willie, however, may have picked up his father's illness. And his scrawny little body just couldn't recover as easily. Edward had said more than once that he and Frances would return to their "western wanderings" when everyone was well. But when would that be with such a sick baby?

What time she did not devote to her family or her artwork, Frances gave willingly to society. Not long ago there had been the young western wife of Governor Dallas to introduce to the city of Montreal. Jane Douglas Dallas and Frances had become fast friends, though their time together had been short. Through Edward, Frances was aware that Jane's father, old Mr. Douglas, had been forced to give up his position with the company. The old man had chosen to become governor of the Colony of Vancouver Island, which was way out on the Pacific coast, and the company could not tolerate such a conflict of interests. While Mr. Douglas' choice of political position had not surprised Edward, the old man's appointing a police force of black men from Jamaica to maintain control of the miners at Fort Victoria had been a controversial one, which her husband did not hesitate to comment upon.

As Della had served tea to Mrs. Dallas, Frances had noticed how much the two dark-eyed beauties resembled one another. Old Mr. Douglas had managed fortunate marriages for his daughters; she wondered for the first time if there would be a man as fine as Mr. Dallas to marry her dear little Della—when it was time.

There was an ever-increasing stream of visitors from abroad: young men from upper-class families with business schemes; politicians for and against incorporating land held by the company into the coming Dominion of Canada; road builders; telegraph engineers; and—other artists. Why, even Governor Dallas had dabbled in watercolor painting, so there was no lack of lively conversation at Hopkins House.

Frances Anne Hopkins, from her very arrival in Montreal, had become one of the city's premier hostesses. On their next trip home (for she and Edward always considered England as home), they would need to hire a butler to keep the house in Côte des Neiges running more smoothly. And they would need to visit their boys. Yes, the boys.

Millie, Della, and often Frances herself spent much of the following winter with the children in their nursery. The room was not large, but it looked out from the second story over the snow-covered garden. Four children in five years required the attention of all three women. Olive was too small to feed herself and Willie was too weak. And, unless supervised, Raymond and Wilfred were too active to pause in their play to eat.

Before spring Baby Willie had nearly stopped eating altogether. Dr. Decker could offer no hope.

"Are we going to lose him?" Millie asked Della when they were alone. "Do you think that tiny blond darling will die?"

Della remembered Mrs. Flynn's prediction two years back. The woman's pessimism had so angered her then. But now she had to admit that the nurse's prediction seemed to be coming true.

As with many Montreal infants that season, the end came quietly. The dear little boy who had always had trouble drawing breath simply stopped breathing. For the Hopkins family, losing Wee Willie was not unexpected. Miss Millie suffered extreme grief and the parents turned to the comfort of each other. The other children were too young to understand the loss of a brother who had seldom been well enough to play with them.

Della wrote a note to her grandmother, though the old lady had never seen the child. In it the saddened girl poured out her heavy heart. She realized that, in a time when cemeteries were dotted with children's graves, the Hopkins were very fortunate to have three healthy young ones and three older boys. Nonetheless, the loss of their precious toddler was heartbreaking.

In early summer the grieving parents had a brief time alone together in the Ottawa District. Though they did not travel by canoe, Frances did prepare a pencil drawing, over which she made a fine watercolor picture. It was a scene at Marquette on the southern shore of Lake Superior—a scene that gave the peace she needed.

Frances was especially fond of the little painting, first because it was a memento of their time together. Then, too, the scene spoke eloquently of the changes coming to the old fur trade routes. There was a large, sturdy house with outbuildings and a plank road along the lakeshore and through the towering trees. With faint hills in the background and rugged shoreline rocks as foreground, it was very much her idea of Canadian scenery. Focusing on her artwork helped ease the pain of her loss.

On August 6th the family departed by company ship for England. Edward needed to rest and they always had family business to attend to with her sisters and his mother, sister, and brothers. And most importantly, they longed to visit their older boys.

While Edward met with company officials, Frances would take one relative or another, most often her widowed sister, Katherine, to the Royal Academy of Arts, which was soon to welcome a number of her paintings.

Although she never admitted to being lonely when the Hopkins family was abroad, Della Macleod soon would find herself in Lachine. Gramma Nell was slowing down and always appreciated what she called an experienced pair of hands in her kitchen. Della could sleep in her own little cot in the cottage she had called home and renew friendships with the other servants and with former class-mates. Several of the girls from her school were married and mothers and, naturally, they asked Della about her own prospects. She was almost embarrassed to admit to them that her life as an individual was almost nonexistent, except when she came back to Lachine.

Della and Abby Ross—the *former* Abby Ross from Montreal, who was now Mrs. Robert Eaton—met for a cup of tea at the old market. "Do you remember Captain Scott?" Abby asked.

For a moment Della did not. Then she said, "Yes, certainly. The young officer Millie was so taken with. He has become a captain, then?"

"Indeed he has. And this is what I wanted to pass along to you. In confidence, of course."

Della nodded, but in so doing, knew that she would say some-thing about this news to Millie at first opportunity.

"Well, Della. Captain Scott has twice asked my Robert if we were in contact with Miss Stapleton. Can you believe that?"

"Yes, I *can* believe that!" Della answered a little too forcefully. "Millie is a wonderful person. She is like a mother to the Hopkins children and they all love her dearly. As do I!" She stopped speaking abruptly, then told Abby that she must get back to help her grand-mother with the evening meal. Della was more than a little piqued with Abby's sharp tongue and thought it best to part while they were still friends.

She didn't have to get back to Gramma at all—at least not this soon. After she was sure Abby had headed home, Della wandered along the main business district looking into shop windows. Years ago she would have felt quite comfortable strolling alone, but now that she was grown up and dressed more as a lady, she became con-scious of the looks being cast her way by some around her.

"And what is a pretty young lady like yourself doing out without your grandma's protection?" a voice said near her ear.

Della jumped away and knocked her shoulder into the window frame, shaking it and herself at the same time.

"Oh, dear. Oh *dear*! Forgive me little Della. I never thought how my words might frighten you."

The Scottish voice was somewhat familiar, but the face was nearly covered by whiskers and the eyes in shadow of a tall silk hat. When the man swept the hat aside, she recognized none other than Mr. Colin Steven, the boys' one-time schoolmaster.

"Why, Mr. Steven. You did give me a start. Do you always creep up on the innocent and unsuspecting and startle them so?"

Now that he had her attention, Mr. Steven found nothing more to say. Della thought she saw more than summer sun coloring his cheeks. They stood open-mouthed and looked at each other. Finally the man said, "It is Miss Macleod, I hope."

Della had to laugh at the look of terror in his eyes. "Yes, Mr. Steven, it's me, Della. I'm very surprised to see that you are still in Lachine after all these years."

"And where would you expect one who will *never* cross another ocean to spend his life?" he asked with a smile of his own. Both were feeling as though they had found an old friend.

"Gramma Nell," Della called, coming in the kitchen door from the sunny garden. "You'll never guess who I met in the town."

"I would guess. And it would be Abby Ross, or whatever name she has now. But I wouldn't be expecting that she would put such color into your cheeks, so maybe you'd better tell me about who else you met."

✳ ✳ ✳

Back at the house in Montreal, a short train ride from Lachine, Della had work to attend. The other staff took time off, too, when the family was absent, but there was always work to be done. Mrs. Roberts, the cook and housekeeper, was somewhat gruff and wielded her power with extra strength when kindly Mrs. Hopkins was not in residence. Della spent afternoons in the garden where she didn't feel so under observation. She sat in the early evenings in Mrs. Hopkins' studio and read the *Montreal Gazette* or wrote short letters to her grandmother. She thought a time or two about Mr. Steven, each time with a mixture of embarrassment and pleasure at their chance meeting. Finally, she admitted to herself that she would be very happy to hear the rooms around her filled with running feet and baby cries once again. And she would be most happy to hear Millie Stapleton giggling in the bed next to hers. All at once, Della realized that she was lonely.

XII

Inviting Pathways

After the sadness of their infant's death in early 1864, Edward and Frances Hopkins drew even closer. In fact, they were seldom parted. When it was necessary for her husband to travel, Frances often accompanied him. Her many friends may have considered such absences from her young children a little selfish of Frances, but some may also have understood her desire to develop artistically. After all, her paintings had been shown in London, and she was fortunate enough to have excellent and reliable staff at the big house in Montreal.

In July the couple journeyed as far as Fort William on the western edge of Lake Superior. This was Edward's tour of inspection and, therefore, basically a business trip. For Frances, however, it was a step back in time.

In their years together Frances had learned much about the history of the company her husband helped to administer. First, of course, the French traders had come through the continent to the area around Fort William, the area that was their destination on this trip. "You will understand, my dear, that just as the rapids near Lachine prompted the founding of both that village and Montreal itself, Kakabeka Falls on the Kaministiquia River and rapids on the Pigeon River further south made this a logical site for a transshipment establishment. And at the time when I entered the trade, Fort

William was an absolute amazement to all who entered here."

"Those original names come lightly from your tongue, husband. And I can see by the condition of these buildings that trade in furs is definitely coming to an end. It is good to know that some memories from the early times—the North American People's names for these places, for example—will remain.

"Yes, the Ojibwe in this area. Oh, but Frances, you should have seen this place three or four decades ago when no penny was spared to bring the best of Europe inside these walls. Why, the wintering partners—they were the North West Company then—had life as good here as did their counterparts on the east coast." And thus, before or after his meetings, Edward would walk the fading pathways of the old fort with his attentive wife and explain the workings of each segment of the operation, from the farm on the west to the fur press to the canoe sheds. On her own, she was free to inspect the various specialty buildings inside the walls. The couple was housed, naturally, within the Great Hall, as visiting dignitaries had always been lodged, and even by the standards of the 1860s, Frances was impressed.

The Great Hall dining room could seat well over a hundred, with space to spare. Before their visit ended, that room was cleared, as it had been in times past, to make room for lively singing and dancing to the music of fiddle, pipe, and drum. For Frances, there was no happier moment than walking arm-in-arm with her husband through the Main Gate to the shore and cooling their glowing faces in the evening breeze off the water.

When they stopped on Lake Superior's south shore, Frances made another good-sized pencil drawing of the plank roadway leading to a lakeside dwelling. Later she would go over the drawing with watercolors, adding the look of summer to the scene. "You never seem to tire of it, do you, my dear," her husband teased. "I believe you might have made a very adequate company partner yourself."

"Voyageur, I'd prefer," Frances teased back. "So as to have all the adventure and none of the responsibility that often troubles you, my dear."

★ ★ ★

In August the family departed for England and was not expected to return until mid-November. With so many weeks to herself, Della thought of spending some time at Lachine. But an encounter on a side street in Montreal Center changed her mind and her life.

Della had accompanied Mrs. Roberts on her weekly grocery shopping trip. Both women carried deep baskets with which to bear home their goods. While Mrs. Roberts went ahead to find her favorite cheese, Della turned into a street she seldom visited: the street of dressmakers. The girl had no need of their services, having become a reasonably accomplished seamstress, but thought it might be fun to compare talents.

In the second shop from the corner stood a small card reading *Design Suggestions Offered.*

Design suggestions? What could that mean? Didn't all professional dressmakers simply refer to the latest fashion magazines from Europe and make copies of those dresses?

The dress displayed on a form to the left of the card answered her question. It was exquisite, one of a kind, unique and extremely beautiful. The fabric must have been silk. It was warm peach in color and trimmed by yards of embroidered tape. The sleeves had the same trim, and the bustle was full over a train of peachy waves.

As Della admired the dress, a face moved on the other side of the window—a familiar face. Could it be? Della held her breath while the form moved to the open doorway.

"On you, mademoiselle, I think—blue."

"Miss Nora?" Della sputtered. "Is it you, Miss Nora?"

"In the flesh, little miss—who isn't so little any longer, I see." The woman's face slowly broke into a smile, possibly the first that Della had ever seen there.

"But, Miss Nora, what are you doing back in Montreal? We heard that you had run off…I mean, that you were living…"

"In Red River or Vancouver with a handsome French Canadian named Denis? All would be true, and such savage places and people I would never want to see again. But, come inside, *cheri*. Let us do—oh, what is that expression? Ah, a little catching up."

Suddenly, Mrs. Roberts' bustling form could be seen at the end of the street. "Are you here often? It would be better if I came another time—when I was alone," Della stammered.

"As it suits you. I am here always. This is my own shop." She added quietly, "I do hope you will come again, Della."

The two had not actually been friends when they worked together in the Hopkins' Lachine house, but each seemed to desire that a friendly relationship be given a chance to develop.

Della was now past eighteen years old and quite independent. Other than the usual mending and repairing, and a bit of help with household duties, she could use her summer hours as she wished.

The Hopkins' nursery was simply too quiet to sit in alone, so she took to spending her mornings in Mrs. Hopkins' studio. Poetry books were the only items there that were not related to drawing or painting.

Mrs. Hopkins would be pleasantly surprised to see Mr. Longfellow's newest publication, *Tales of a Wayside Inn*, sitting beside *Evangeline* and *Hiawatha* and *Miles Standish*. Della had used her own money to buy the new volume and she was glad that she had. Since it was her own book, she would never have to be far from the tall, thin, blue-eyed, yellow-haired Norwegian musician. Della couldn't quite decide if it was the man (imaginary though he was) or his Viking stories (ancient as they were) that thrilled her more, but she began to dream of brave blond men.

Sometimes, however, she would put down that poetry book and

take up a bit of pencil and play with making her own dress designs. Since seeing the gown in Miss Nora's window, she could draw no other. Her dresses weren't as frilly-gorgeous as the original, but much more practical for young women of her station.

Only a few days after meeting Miss Nora, Della had drawn a pleasing version of the peachy dress. As Nora had said, Della thought of it in blue. So, then, why shouldn't her drawing be made in blue?

No one touched Mrs. Hopkins' paints. No one. But since Della had been allowed free access to the studio, she didn't really think Frances would mind if she used just a touch of the blue watercolor. Just a bit. She located paper that had been set aside for the children's use and by folding a larger sheet in the middle, formed a container—was portfolio the word?—for her first designs.

Della found opportunity to visit Miss Nora's shop again. She wore a blue cotton version of the lovely peach frock that was still displayed in Nora's window. Della had fashioned a little bonnet, trimmed with fabric matching her dress, and she carried, hidden away in a matching carry-bag, her little portfolio.

Miss Nora was busy with customers, a matron and her daughters of about ten and twelve years of age. The girls were round-faced and round-bodied, the type of figure most young ladies had before they became young women.

Della pretended interest in the fine brocade and delicate silk samples neatly displayed on a cutting table. Nora was saying, "…and in just a year or two, Mrs. Brock, they will surely be ready for a ball gown neckline, but until then, I would truly recommend keeping the bodice gently scooped and the waist as smooth as possible. Not time just yet to show shoulders."

Della wondered why a mother would want the shoulders of girls that age to be shown—and where? But, then, she was a maid and a Canadian and she realized that her values were somewhat more *reserved* than were those of Montreal's wealthy matrons.

Before long Della and Nora were alone and talking as easily as though four years had not passed. "That must have been a sample of 'design suggestions,'" Della teased.

"But of course, *cheri*. The first lesson of business: Give the customer what she wants. Or in that case, what she will come to be happy with." They laughed together. "I was able to convince Madame Brock that her little round daughters should not wear big round skirts. Their mother, of course, insists on wearing six-tier, eighteen-foot-wide cage crinoline hoopskirts herself. Madame prides herself on displaying her husband's wealth and prestige in this community with the size of her hoopskirts! But since she comes to me for them, will I complain?" The two laughed compatibly.

Feeling more confident of Nora's acceptance, Della bravely placed her designs on the table. These gowns were as nothing compared to what Nora dealt in, but they were attractive, serviceable dresses for working women like herself. "You see by my drawing, Nora, that I have somewhat revised the enormous and terribly impractical hoopskirts. For such as myself, who actually must work with an efficiency of movement, I have designed a different type of hoop. Here. I have made a drawing of it also."

The page showed what looked like a rounded birdcage with a flat side. "Millie and I have never worn the six-bone crinolines, as Mrs. Hopkins and her lady friends use with their fancy gowns. The weight of the whalebone forms is simply too great to carry all day. And notice here—just as you told that customer a moment ago—I have kept the front of the cage flat so that the wearer can get nearer the child or the sewing machine or whatever work needs doing without destroying the household china in the process. Using a term I learned at school, I call this an *elliptical* cage."

Nora was impressed—or said that she was. "The problem," she

explained, "is obtaining the cotton fabric. Since this dreadful war in the States, it is next to impossible to obtain enough fabric, either from New England mills or from those in Old England."

Della had not considered the economic impact of that awful war. She reminded herself that she must spend more time reading the news and less thinking about the poetic Norwegian.

"To be honest, young miss, I am most impressed with these bonnets you have shown to accompany your designs. Have you continued your interest in fashioning ladies' headwear?"

Della blushed. She was, in fact, quite proud that Mrs. Hopkins now wore her creations exclusively. And Della had even been commissioned to make fancy hats for two lady friends of Mrs. Hopkins. Frances, it seemed, was quite proud to have another woman artist in her household. Her answer to Nora, however, was a simple, "Yes. Sometimes I try my hand at constructing what I draw."

When the Hopkins family returned, Millie nearly burst before evening came and she and Della could be alone in their room. Della, too, had exciting news to share, but the vivacious Millie blurted out, even before their door had closed, "Della! We came home on *his* ship!" There was no need to ask who *he* was. In any case, Millie spent the next half-hour relating what was said and what looks were given and what future arrangements had been hinted at by the most handsome and charming, if somewhat shy, Captain Alan Scott of the HBC ship *Princess Royal*. Millie didn't stop speaking until she was literally out of breath.

Della's news paled by comparison. What did it matter to a woman in love that her roommate had been asked to become actively involved in a Montreal ladies' apparel business.

XIII

For the Birds

"Della? Della Macleod. Is that you scampering past my door?"

This could mean trouble. Mrs. Hopkins never raised her voice. Della set a basket of the children's newly mended playclothes on the back stairway and walked slowly to the studio door. Was the blue paint going to become a problem?

"Come in, Della, and sit there. No. No, that will not do. Would you mind letting your hair down?"

Della was completely bewildered. "What is it, Mrs. Hopkins? Have I done something to displease you? Well, Yes, I surely have, but..." She was unwinding the bun of heavy black hair from her neck. She tipped her head back and shook the tresses free.

"No. Not so much. Let it fall naturally," Frances said. "Leave it a little pulled back from your face. Yes, now tuck the left side behind your ear. Yes. Very good. Now you may sit again."

Suddenly Della realized what all this was about. "I'm to be a model, then?" she asked.

"Yes, indeed you are. And just to tease those younger sisters of mine who have begun calling me Canoe Lady!" Frances actually laughed at the thought.

"You see, Della...oh, how should I put this so that you will understand? My sisters are of the opinion that my paintings are too...wild.

They think no one will ever want to display a canoe in their parlor. They said during my last visit home that, if I am to have work displayed 'on the line,' which means in the most desirable placement in an exhibition, then the subject will need to be more *in line* with current—oh, I suppose it would be called romantic sentimentality.

"They could just be correct in that opinion, though. As exciting as I believe log rafts and canoe trips to be, my sisters want something, well…serene. And stepping in here just now, I believe I have found a very appropriate subject: Longfellow!"

Now Della was confused again. "You want *me* to pose as Mr. Longfellow?" she asked in amazement.

This time Frances did actually laugh—a full, hearty sound. "Oh, Della. Dear girl. I am not making much sense, am I?" Frances held her sketchbook before Della. There, already, was a birch bark canoe just waiting an occupant. "I want you to sit as Minnehaha! How many times have we read her sadly beautiful story right here in this studio? We both have admired in that young wife the combination of strength and gentleness, as did her husband, Hiawatha. To say nothing of half the world who have bought copies of Mr. Longfellow's poem.

"I'm going to show my sisters that a canoe, painted with authority, can indeed be as beautiful as a poem. The poem which suggested it. Now, Della, if you would do one more thing to assist me."

"Yes, of course, Mrs. Hopkins. You need only ask."

The assignment was certainly not an easy one. Even when completed, she was not sure she had been successful. Fortunately, as was generally the case, many other family and social matters intervened before the artist asked if Della's work had been finished.

What the artist received from Della was a list of words arranged alphabetically:

blue heron	goose	owl	plover	seagull	whippoorwill
bluebird	grouse	pelican	raven	swallow	woodpecker
eagle	loon	pigeon	robin	swan	

"My dear Della," Frances exclaimed. "I had no idea there would be so many birds mentioned in that poem! Yet, perhaps unconsciously that is what moved me to compose *Minnehaha Feeding Birds*! You have done an excellent job. Thank you. Thank you very much, dear Della."

"But how will you ever choose which birds Minnehaha will be feeding?" Della asked.

"That should not be too difficult," came the answer. "They must be small enough to sit on the side of her canoe. And, you know something, Della? I'll wager Minnehaha would not at all mind being called Canoe Lady!"

"But names are important," Della said a little hesitantly. "At least for us they are. Perhaps you could think more of the *Lady* part of that name. That part certainly suits you well enough."

"You are a sweet one, Della. Thank you. But while we work today, I would like to concentrate on this young *native* woman. Why don't you help me by—oh, by telling me—yes, tell me about your own name. I understand from your grandmother that the Isobel part has been included in your women's line for several generations. Could you tell me about that while I paint?"

As she often did while working, Frances pointed the tip of her paintbrush with her mouth, then poised it before the canvas. Moments passed before Della began. Strangely, she was not sure if she should be sharing what she knew of the first Isobel with the wife of an important company officer.

"It's just an old family story," she began. "My mother and Gramma and her mother—I don't know how many women back—took the name Isobel to honor a woman who lived here and worked for the company a long time ago. I don't think 'lady' would be any part of her name because she pretended to be a man."

"Oh, my!" Frances said, and re-pointed her brush. "And you say she *worked* here in Canada—maybe a hundred years ago? I didn't think there were many of my country-women in Canada at that time. Not *working* in any case. How very intriguing!"

"Well, Mrs. Hopkins, Gramma would be able to tell you more. I only know that one of my ancestors named Annie McGrath was first to add Isobel to her name, and we have continued the tradition ever since. So here am I: Della Isobel Minnehaha." They shared the laughter.

Of all the paintings that Della saw Frances compose (and there would be many, many others that the girl would never see), *Minnehaha Feeding Birds* would be her favorite. Naturally, she was especially proud to have *her* image as the Indian woman from Longfellow's *Song of Hiawatha. Her* picture was golden. It had a soft summer morning atmosphere and a warmth both in locale and subject matter.

Minnehaha Feeding Birds
Frances Ann Hopkins, oil on canvas.
Minnesota Historical Society, St. Paul, Minnesota.

84

The artist had borrowed an authentic North American doeskin dress from her husband's collection. Before slipping it over her head, Della asked, "Do you mind if I keep my shift on under it, Mrs. Hopkins? I had no idea how such an item, when old and creased, would chafe the skin."

Della wore her own blue bead necklace, but Frances asked her to turn the intricate design to the back because she preferred the simplicity of a single strand of beads at the neckline.

Also from Edward's collection they took a birch bark basket, which Della held in her left hand and from which she offered imaginary food to imaginary birds with her outstretched right hand.

Selection of just the right birds was a special memory for Della and probably for the little Hopkins boys, Raymond and Wilfred.

Remembering the delightful day that the older boys had had seeing canoe building first hand, Edward had suggested to Frances that they make another family outing to decide which birds should be painted with Minnehaha. Della was happy to be included in their plan to travel by train to Lachine. However, she did not accompany the family along the St. Lawrence shoreline. She had family of her own to visit, and a very important reason for doing so.

During the years that she had lived in Montreal, Della had not often seen her father and brothers. A time or two when Della was there, Gramma Nell had allowed the twins to overnight at her cottage, but connections were difficult to arrange, especially when Della's free hours were never certain. This time, though, Della had gone to great trouble to arrange that her father and the boys should meet her at the Old Stone Warehouse on the canal. She had also made a midday appointment with the HBC doctor there.

Her brothers were half-grown now at nearly twelve years old.

Certainly they showed none of the hesitations and embarrassments that Della had felt at that age. But today she was more interested in what was—or wasn't—inside the twins.

During one of their painting sessions, Della had entertained Mrs. Hopkins with a hilarious account of the day all of the girls at her school had been vaccinated against smallpox. Since this medical procedure was a requirement for continued attendance at the school, there was no way out for a weak-hearted girl.

Della, herself, had always admired and completely trusted the good Sisters of Saint Anne. These women helped each girl roll up the left sleeve of her long black uniform and bare her upper arm for the needles. However, when the girl in line in front of her fainted and the girl behind her threw up, Della had begun to wonder what they knew about the pain involved in becoming vaccinated that she did not know.

She had concluded her amusing story with a sober statement of personal worry: her young brothers had never received that protective vaccine. Della's eyes misted when she and Frances discussed the possible causes of native people becoming so much more seriously ill from smallpox epidemics than did latecomers to North America. No one had an answer as to why a larger percentage of those people died when compared with a European population likewise infected.

Perhaps because Frances had lost her own little boy, she said to the girl who had posed so perfectly, "Della, would you allow Mr. Hopkins and me to have the company doctor inoculate your brothers, as a kind of thank-you for Minnehaha?"

So, the day for bird-watching and inoculations had arrived. And at last, walking along the canal were Bobby and Johnny, like bookends on either side of their tall father.

While Dr. Thomas performed his needlework on the brave boys—boys who had suddenly become children again—Papa spoke seriously with Della.

"*Ma petite*, you can see from both sides how the company is changing. My services are more for entertainment now than for fur trade transport." What Big Louie did not mention was that, at age thirty-seven, his time as bowsman was also coming to an end.

Her father continued, "Since their mother left us, I have been looking into taking the boys west with me, Della. Maybe even as far as Red River of the North. There is still work in that area and many of our people have settled in the valley."

Della's rounded mouth and her wide eyes showed her emotion. "But, Papa…" she began.

"Do you think I would allow Dr. Thomas to hurt my sons even with a little prick in the arm if it were not for good reason? The pox sickness can still be found in the North West. I will not take those boys into trouble."

Years later, they would all find that Trouble was exactly what they would travel into.

XIV

A Familiar Road

"Frances, Frances dear?" Edward Hopkins came bursting into the back parlor and asked, "Della, where is my good wife? In her studio, as usual, I suppose."

"She is, sir. But I believe she is at the arduous task of preparing canvas, not actually painting."

That evening Millie reported an overheard conversation to Della. "I know I should not have eavesdropped, but—well, he didn't even shut the door, and after all this concerns my future, too. And yours, Della."

Della replied, "I heard, too, Millie, but not because I tried to. I don't understand, though, what Mr. Hopkins' being elected to some London Reform Club has to do with our future—or futures."

"Oh, Della, you can be such a child! All right! I'll explain my concern. If Mr. Hopkins has applied and been elected to membership in a club of such high standing, that means that sooner rather than later he will be retiring from the company and we will all be going back home—permanently. Well, not you, Della. But the babies and—us."

They sat in shocked silence for considerable time. At last Della said, "Then you know what we must do, Miss Millie." There was no answer and none expected. "It is time we grew up," Della said quietly.

* * *

Growing up didn't take Millie long at all. By the end of summer 1865, she was engaged to be married. "He has proposed by post! Can you believe it, Della? Can you see me, simple Millie Stapleton, becoming Mrs. Captain Alan Scott?"

The summer had been another busy one, with much travel both within Canada and across the Atlantic. Neither young woman understood, nor did they want to, the increasing economic complications of the HBC in Canada.

Edward thought it necessary to reply in person and *in London* to criticism of his business operations in the Montreal Department of HBC. In early March, with two little boys and a toddling baby girl, they made the now routine steamship crossing to England.

At the school in Sussex, they were reunited with their older boys: Gouverneur, fifteen; Ogden, thirteen; and Manley, twelve. Then Frances and the younger children encamped again with Aunt Katherine Hopkins. During this visit an additional relative made the rounds of visits with aunties. Edward's twenty-one-year-old nephew, Gerard Manley Hopkins, spent a good deal of time with Aunt Frances and Aunt Katherine.

Gerard was a student at Oxford. He seemed to enjoy the company of the Beechey/Hopkins sisters and often visited with them to share his deep thoughts, his drawings, and his poetry. Edward's handsome godson was a welcome diversion for Frances, but he worried the older Aunt Kate.

"Well, Frances Anne. Wouldn't you worry if one of your boys was keeping company with a crowd who wanted to reunite the Anglican Church with the Church of Rome?"

"Are you saying that Gerard is interested in Catholicism?" asked Frances in alarm. "I thought his major interest lay in the classics and in writing poetry."

"If you ask me," fumed the emotional Katherine, "his major interest should be in a woman! Oh, dear, I should not have said that,

Fanny, but he is so up one day and down the next. No wonder the family is worried! Poor appetite, worse digestion when he does eat. The boy is showing very—very eccentric ways. The family is at a loss as to what to think. Has Edward mentioned none of this to you?"

"You press me to remind you, sister, that Edward's attention must needs be elsewhere. The once all-powerful Hudson's Bay Company is no longer seeing the profits of the past, which, of course, affects our own personal income. Not only that, but with this talk of confederation in Canada and with native unrest in the west…never would I add an extra burden to my husband's load."

Although the future priest and poet Gerard Manley Hopkins did continue to call, the sisters did not discuss his "unacceptable" religious leanings again.

Nor did Aunt Kate share with Aunt Frances the fact that she had gladly chaperoned Cousin Millie at tea with a timid company ship captain named Alan Scott. After all, it had been the bride-to-be, Katherine, who had encouraged young Millie to leave the country farm and it was now Katherine, the widow, who wished only happiness for a woman so obviously in love.

✶ ✶ ✶

By June everyone was back in Montreal, but only briefly. Edward sat on the inn's veranda beside his wife as she sketched a hillside in South Bolton. He did not consider this view a scene worth remembering, but said nothing. He supposed his dear wife was again recording dramatic changes of the landscape made in the name of progress.

During this trip alone together, they again discussed Frances' desire to accompany him more often into the wilderness. The denuded and burnt forests before them—the picture she was drawing—presented the strongest argument. Earlier that month, and under similar artistic circumstances, Frances had listened silently while making a drawing of their Côte des Neiges' house. A case was being made to Edward that he, being among the last high-ranking HBC officers to know the old canoe route between Lake Huron and Ottawa, should accompany Sir John Michel and Sir James Hope on an inspection tour of Canada's defenses.

At Edward's suggestion, Frances had Della bring into their garden a rather large watercolor entitled *Paquanah, Morning Mist* which had been completed a couple of years back.

"As you see, gentlemen," Edward said to Sir John and Sir James, "my wife is not only an exceptionally hearty canoe traveler, but an excellent artist. If suddenly we notice that she has gone missing from camp, we need only check the high places nearby to find her sitting with sketchbook and pencil in hand. The result, displayed here, allows you to see that she is often the first to be up of a morning and the last to have her precious cargo loaded."

"When you say 'her cargo,' may I inquire, Mrs. Hopkins, do you take canvas and easel along, or merely sketchbook?" Sir James, like many military men of the time, was somewhat an artist himself.

There followed a lively discussion, not unfamiliar to a woman who had grown up amid artists. "Yes, I have a small wooden box of watercolors which I generally bring along, but actually prefer just my pencil and sketchbook." By close of the afternoon, both guests were convinced of the near photographic exactness of their hostesses' work. In addition, they marveled that her husband not only encouraged her inland travel, but, it seemed, strongly approved her pursuit of the canoe voyage scene as focus for her obvious artistic ability.

This time, however, the answer from Edward was *no*. The military would not welcome a woman along, no matter her talent or her husband's distinguished position in the company.

Several days later Frances joined her husband in the parlor. She carried a business letter just taken from its envelope. "Edward, the London gallery has sold two more of my Canadian pictures!" She did not add that both paintings had been purchased by the same person or that the buyer was a former company officer who could appreciate the subject matter. It was enough for her to know that there *were* those among gallery crowds who saw merit in her art work. "Thank you, my dear husband for your support and for—oh, Edward—for your canoes!"

But sometimes Frances became a little depressed by all the changes happening around her. Edward suggested that she should then concentrate on capturing what he called "a vision from the past."

"Since you have brought up the past, husband, I have a question about that shadowy time."

Edward smiled invitingly. He enjoyed storytelling and history, which to him were one and the same. Frances continued, "Our Della was telling me about a woman named Isobel who, pretending to be a man, once worked for the company." She stopped abruptly, noting that Edward's smile had faded completely.

"The company does not speak of that unfortunate incident. Nor do I," he said firmly.

Frances decided thereafter that it would be best to confine her "visions of the past" to her artwork. This she did one spring morning in 1866.

In preparation for the summer tour of inspection, which Edward had promised that she could make with him, Frances, her two young ladies and the three children were spending time nearly every day in their walking boots.

While Olive was no longer a baby, neither could she keep up with her big brothers. When the little girl tired, each of the women took her up in turn. Finally, when all of them were flagging, they sat beside the roadway.

Never without her sketchbook, Frances began to draw the small house in whose yard they were resting. They all had seen the place countless times because it stood on the Lachine Road. Its distinguishing features were a tall cross beside a wooden well. Neither of these articles was unique, nor was the dwelling. They were simply representative of the French-Catholic influence in the area. But the combination of house, cross, and well composed a natural, well-balanced picture in itself.

Frances sketched hastily, as she always did when especially excited by the subject. When the housewife came to the doorstep to ask if they would like a drink from her well, Raymond proudly showed the woman his mother's drawing. Refreshed and happy, the little group started back in the direction from which they had come.

"Could we have a song, Della?" Raymond asked. "A soldier song, please?"

"Will you be a soldier, Raymond? I'm afraid I don't know any songs for a soldier, but certainly some for a voyageur. Shall we try the best known of all?" And here they began immediately into French: *"Alouette, gentille alouette; Alouette, je t'y plumerai."*

XV

A Rose and a Barrel

At last, at last! Frances Anne Hopkins was in her element—inland Canada by way of canoe. She had, indeed, become the Canoe Lady. These summer excursions were no longer fur trading trips as in the earlier sense. Now they were pleasure (or memory) trips of inspection for Edward, and, as he had promised, sketchbook fillers for his artist wife.

They traveled in two or three birch bark canoes manned by six to eight voyageurs each. By now Mr. Hopkins' wife was an old hand at canoe travel and river camping. She and Edward had a white canvas tent high enough in the middle for her to stand up in and wide enough for their canvas cots. Thanks to Edward's rank, the couple wanted for very little in the wilderness that they did not also have at home in Montreal: warm wool blankets, feather pillows, a tin lantern with tallow candles, and tin plates, cups, and eating utensils. There was even a glass decanter for evening brandy, which might help a tired body to sleep soundly.

The voyageurs, if they could be called that now that their only cargo was human, were known to Frances and, while they seldom traveled with women, certainly not European women, they admired her artistic talent and her physical stamina. In addition to paddling forty to fifty strokes per minute and singing melodiously all the while on water, and in addition to unloading, carrying, and reloading the trunks, barrels, and boxes that contained the comforts of home, these men were virtual servants to the chief factor and his wife. While Edward had, from earliest encounter, held such laborers in high regard, Frances, too, appreciated their attentiveness. While it was necessary to dismantle the canvas tent first thing each morning so that its five long poles could be placed in the bottom of the birch bark canoe, this task was never begun until Madame Hopkins herself removed whatever articles of clothing might be drying on the tent's support ropes.

Except while eating, Mrs. Hopkins was never without a sketchbook or poetry book in hand. She and Edward were quite comfortable side-by-side in the middle position of their craft. They sat on "trade" blankets, the same that would warm them at night, and leaned against backrests especially designed to ease the strain of long lake crossings.

Frances never lacked colorful entertainment. Her companions themselves were a source of hours of humorous paddle songs and stories, though, of course, these were presented in a revised and polite version that would be suitable for the Canoe Lady, as the men thought of her.

Along a lakeshore in early September, the men had been singing a lively song in French: *"Lui y a longtemps que je t'aime; Jamais je ne t'oublierai."*

Frances had been intently sketching the shoreline and listened only to the heavy beat of what she thought of as the stroke chorus. "Do you know this one, my dear?" asked Edward. "It was the very first in my collection of voyageur paddle songs."

When the bowsman called for a "smoke" or rest period, Frances asked Edward, knowing that he was very proud of his paddle songs, "Were they singing about a barrel? Sorry, dear. I wasn't actually paying attention to the words."

"A barrel?" Edward laughed and turned to the *gouvernail*, or steersman, standing behind him. "No, but there is a good story about a barrel. Martin LeBec, would you care to explain the story of Mr.

Barrel to my wife? We will leave the boy in the last song—who lost his love over a bouquet of roses, my dear—for another time."

The steersman, who stood at the stern of the canoe during every moment but smoke-time, squatted now and smiled mischievously at their lady passenger.

"But of course, sir. And a better story it is." LeBec took his red knit hat from his sweating head and removed his pipe and fixings from the folded upper flap. He cut tobacco from the twisted plug and slowly filled his pipe. "You have heard of the North West Company, madame?" he began.

"Yes," Frances said, "the rival Scots traders who became partners with our own company." She looked to her husband for confirmation.

"That is correct, my dear. Long before my time, that was. Eighteen twenty-one, in fact. So this story took place some fifty years ago, if it happened at all."

"Oh, yes, Mr. Hopkins. I believe it to be true," said LeBec earnestly. "There are so many of my cousins who have told me of it."

Murmurings of, "Yes, yes. It happened as they say, Mr. Hopkins," came from other positions in the still canoe.

"Well, then, madame," Martin began:

There is a portage on the Winnipeg River far to the west. It is called Baril Portage, which of course in the English sounds like "barrel"—the cask or keg which we use for transporting some foods and liquids.

Martin LeBec paused to puff at his clay pipe. Frances knew that the telling of the story—the style of the teller—was considered as important as the tale itself. She waited patiently.

So—there were good men like us from this company working the way west in brigade. It being to the west, we—they—carried a year's supply of trade goods. There was cloth and iron pots, knives and axes, blankets and sewing needles. And…and, of course, rum. Men at the rear of our company reported, about the time they had reached the Winnipeg, that a brigade of the North West Company was not many days behind them. Those days, madame, before we two companies joined together, were not always pleasant days and good feelings between the companies were not easy to find.

"A major reason for the forced merger," Edward whispered in his wife's ear. LeBec continued, his words picking up speed as his canoe might do when it reached a west-flowing river:

The partner, whose name has not come along with the story—and maybe for good reason—feared, madame, that his keg of rum would be stolen by the brigade behind, which was reported to outnumber his group in manpower. So—what do you think? What do you think he did? Yes! He ordered a hole to be dug along the portage trail and they buried Mr. Keg. But, madame, they did not call him that name. *No!* These ingenious men named him Monsieur Baril: Mr. Barrel! *Yes!* They put him into the ground as though he had died while carrying too much weight over the portage. To make it even better, they erected a cross, on which they wrote: *A La Memoire de Monsieur Baril.* Do you think, madame, that even the cruel men of the North West Company would disturb such a grave?

Of course not!

But, madame, when my cousins returned over that portage at the close of summer, struggling under their many loads of the finest beaver pelts, do you think *they* did not disturb the remains of Monsieur Baril? Of course they did! And, madame, they drank—with many a laugh—the good health of their friend, Monsieur Baril!

There were cheers all around for Mr. Barrel and for Martin LeBec's story. And though she had never wondered why Edward made his tours of inspection in this old-fashioned mode of travel, Frances knew positively now that he was still drawn to the camaraderie of the men of the brigades. Edward, and now she, appreciated their achievements through teamwork; she understood the discipline that must attend such responsibility with lives and goods. She was aware deep in her artistic being that it was the *collective enterprise* of these men that must be remembered for the success of the famed Hudson's Bay Company of Canada.

Frances filled her sketchbooks (and her mind) with canoes and their occupants. She recorded many aspects of everyday voyageur life. There were small pencil sketches of their camping sites, and pen and ink drawings when she could sit down on shore and depict their laborious portages. She drew their tents, their equipment—pots, pans, and paddles. She showed the canoes in and out of water. She drew the individual faces of men she had come to admire, dirty and smelly though they might be. She knew without conscious thought that her very life was in the hands of these men who were called Canadians. They were as rugged and as colorful as their country and sometimes as wild. And she would paint exactly what she saw. Her work would be realistic and for her own family if buyers could not be found who were interested in the subjects to which she and her husband were so attracted.

By their return to Ottawa, Frances Anne Hopkins, artist, was quite satisfied with her storehouse of sketches for future work. The late summer inspection tour had been a complete success. As reward to herself and Edward, they went boating on the Ottawa River under the bluff of the new parliament buildings. In the picture that she completed a year later, she would show the two of them in a small day boat near the shore opposite the castle-like towers of the government buildings. When her sisters criticized her for having included a timber raft in the background of such a fairytale painting, she told them simply, "That is Canada. I painted exactly what I saw."

XVI

Packing Up

"…So, my people from across the river captured the eight-hundred-pound bell from the people in Deerfield, which is south in Massachusetts." Della glanced at Millie, but couldn't determine her reaction to the story. "Then after many 'trials and tribulations,' as Mr. Steven would say, they carried it, yes, *carried* it back here to Caughnawaga for the people who had rightfully paid a French city for it in the first place." Another pause to look at her work partner. "This happened very long ago in our history—I will say, oh, seventeen hundred and something and…Millie, are you listening? You asked me to tell you about the bell we are hearing. Millie?"

"Sometimes I feel that she just doesn't love these children as much as she did Edward's boys when they were the same ages."

Della raised her eyebrows, then closed her eyes and shook her head, at last understanding the sudden shift in direction. "Oh how silly, Millicent Stapleton! These *are* Edward's boys—and girl." Della passed a knit jumper to Millie, who nearly threw it into the steamer trunk they were packing. They had opened the upper window and though it wasn't yet warm, the June air coming in from the St. Lawrence River was fresh and the sound of the Caughnawaga bell pleasingly clear.

Della continued, "You are right about the ages, though. When you and I met, the three older boys were about the ages of these three younger ones now." They sat for a moment, one on each of the small beds. "Don't you wish you could see into the future, Millie? It would be so nice to know if Mrs. Hopkins' beautiful pictures will be, as she puts it, 'well received' by those who attend this summer's Royal Society Exhibition in London." Della paused. "You never say if *you* like the pictures, Millie. Do you?"

"You shouldn't ask *me*, Della. You know more about her art than I do. You are the other artist who puts together fancy feathers and lace and sells them to *Madame Nora* for her hoity-toity customers."

Della reached across and took Millie's fisted hand. "What is it, Millie? What has you so upset?"

The older girl sighed. "Sometimes I don't even know myself," she said. "I love these little ones as though they were my own. In many ways I *am* their mother. But, Della, they are *not* mine and if things don't change soon, I'll be too old to ever have little babies of my own!"

So—that was it, Della thought. She's missing the captain. Every time they make a crossing—one direction or the other—Millie becomes agitated. Will she see him? Will her family, or his, again urge her to leave her position and remain "at home"? What will she do with herself this visit? Six months in London: not really governess and not really free, either. Not married, but spoken for. And when Mr. and Mrs. Hopkins continued on to France, Millie would have full responsibility for their children right there in the midst of all those aunties. No, it was not easy to be twenty-five years old and so—so between one life and another.

Neither was it easy to be twenty years old, a beautiful French-Canadian North American, and unmarried. Della opened Millie's moist fist and squeezed her hand. "Don't worry, dear Millie. I can't see the future, but I feel just *sure* that we will both find our places in it."

✴ ✴ ✴

As they had done with the older boys, Edward and Frances paid considerable attention to the young ones' education. Millie was a natural-born teacher, and though the younger boys did not benefit from anyone as inspiring as Mr. Steven, they had their own tutors soon enough.

Frances encouraged all three children at their drawing, using her own work for their models. Canoes were not easy to execute, but Raymond became quite good at log rafts. Always he included smoke from a fire aboard the logs because he found it so intriguing that the timber rafters could have a fire, yet not set alight their own raft. The boy's cant hooks were often larger than the logs they were attempting to gather in, but he was getting better at showing the shore reflected in water, as his mother was so fond of doing.

Little Wilfred was more interested in things on shore. "Mamma," he would ask, "what makes the cook pot stay between the three cook poles?" Or, "Why do the men carry the tracking rope *under* their arm? I would rather put it over my shoulder and pull, like this."

Even Olive was observant. She would point a baby finger, especially at the larger drawings and say, "Man, man, man. Papa. *Where is my Mama?*" because little Olive always supposed that when Mamma went away, it was to be in the canoes.

Their mamma encouraged the children sincerely with words, but it was Millie who did the hugging and patting.

June through December. *June through December!* What *am* I going to do with so much time? Della had decided not to stay in Montreal while the family was away. She could have stayed and worked more closely with Nora, but some of Millie's restlessness seemed to have rubbed off on her. She wanted to *do* something. And she did not want to spend any more time than necessary under the direction (or in the company!) of the butler, Duncan Wall. The unmarried, middle-aged butler had joined the household some years back and had always made Della uneasy.

"Wall," Mr. Hopkins called him, but Millie and Della, acting the giddy girls they sometimes were, called him Wally when they were alone. Wall was a true and proper, stuffy British butler. Never had he overstepped his authority, nor had he done anything else improper—as far as Della knew. But the *feeling* in the house changed when it was so empty. Della simply did not feel comfortable with Wall. Therefore, she moved home to Lachine, thinking that it would be for six months. It was not.

Within the week, Bobby and Johnny were at Gramma Nell's door.

"You could come with us, Della," they chorused. "It would be a family migration—just like the old people used to do."

"I don't think the old folks moved quite *that* far," Della teased. "And I'll bet you only want me along to cook!"

"Well, sister, isn't that what the women always did?" asked Johnny.

"At least you wouldn't have to trot along the bank, collecting food," Bobby teased.

"I don't know why I told them I would even *consider* going," Della told her grandmother that evening. "What business do I have running off to Red River for the summer? And it's been a long time since I have looked like *or* acted like a native, thanks to my father's educational generosity."

"There you have it all together. Your business in going is *family*. You must know, sweet one, that this will be the last you see of those boys. And possibly Big Louie, too. They will stay out west where being—well, the people we are—is more, I will say, acceptable. While you and I have lived *in* the white community, we have not been part of it. Do you understand what I am telling you, girl? Yes, this is a journey you *should* take into the past. But know also—your other life and I will be right here when you return."

✶ ✶ ✶

"We will travel very light, as in the days before the company arrived to burden us so. You may have with you two small string bags, but they must hang across your upper body so that both hands are free when we portage. And, *ma petite*, I wish for you to wear pants." At Della's look of surprise, he said, "Trousers, like the boys. Unlike your good lady, Mrs. Hopkins, you will not be a passenger, but a—yes—a voyageur!" Her father laughed at his own joke.

Della, with Gramma Nell's support, had become excited by the prospects of this family trip through the wilderness. It could be like one of Mr. Longfellow's romantic poems, only *real*. Already, in her mind, she pictured her pattern for muslin bloomers adapted into good, heavy pantaloons. Yes, she could do it.

"May we make a trade then, Papa? I would like the boys to speak English rather than French during our travels. I know, they use a little now, but I have read that the further west you go, the more English is used. Is that not so, Papa?"

"I will agree to that arrangement for both of your brothers—but it will be up to *you* to see that it happens," he answered with a knowing smile.

Della placed on her little cot the things she thought she would take to Red River:

Two old, but still colorful, cotton blouses
Two pairs of newly made pantaloons
Walking shoes, well broken in by her outings with Mrs. H.
One serviceable cotton day-dress, blue of course
Two sets of undergarments—chemise and bloomers
Two pairs of black hose
One black wool jacket, rugged, but not mannish

Now she needed assistance from Gramma.

"What did Papa mean by string bags, Gramma? Like the one I used to keep my dolls in?"

"Exactly," her grandmother answered. "That one was, as a matter of historic fact, *my* grandmother's. She was Iroquois, you know, but had learned many things from neighboring peoples."

"Maybe she learned something easy for the other question I must ask." There was no hesitation or embarrassment about anything so natural. "What did traveling women do when it came to their time of the moon?"

"Dear child, there was and *is* nothing easy about that. So, they did nothing so very different from ordinary. Drink more water, I might say. And I would suggest that you take all *new* flannel rags along, as it is the repeated washings of those soiled rags which wears them thin so quickly."

Now, Della thought, she was ready. Her efforts would have been completed sooner had she returned to Montreal and used her sewing machine. But her pantaloons in solid blue and solid rusty-brown cotton would surely hold their stitches and she had included in her "necessary" bag an emergency sewing kit. She and Nell surveyed the piles.

"What is missing?" Nell asked.

"Well, there must be something or you wouldn't ask," Della said.

"If you don't know, there will be one *avant* who would not claim you as a bowsman's daughter. Think, girl!"

Finally, Nell had to point to Della's feet. "Moccasins!" the girl cried. "Papa would be so disappointed if I were to wear these heavy-heeled shoes in his canoe!"

"Take new moccasins. The kind that tie above the ankle," Gramma advised. "Get two pair from old Auntie Netta down by the dock. And be sure she gives you plains-buffalo soles. 'Cause that's where you'll be wearin' them."

XVII

Mixed History

The Macleod Brigade, as the twins called their adventure, was seven days out from Lachine. Della was still alive, but wondering how she had managed. Her bottom had been the first to tell her that she had, indeed, been living a soft life. Her neck and shoulders screamed their discomfort throughout the first few nights of the trip. Louie had insisted that, for warmth—until she got used to it—she must sleep between the twins and under the upturned canoe.

"That will help your body to remember that it is one of us again," her father teased.

As far as she could tell, the only other concession they had made for her was a piece of oiled canvas that she was to lie on with her extra blanket.

Della had used her cedar paddle well throughout the first day on the Ottawa River. Even the second strenuous day had gone well enough. But by the third afternoon, after several portages, walking over worn, stony trails, she was beginning to wonder if joining the Macleod Family Wanderers was such a wonderful way to spend the summer after all. She felt very much like crying from the exertion. However, seeing that her younger brothers were doing at least as well as she was, she dared not give over to "being a girl."

They had started out on the last Monday in June. "It's late," Big

Louie had told Gramma Nell. "But since we won't be making the eastward segment—except one of us by steam and rail—this time the seasons won't matter."

★ ★ ★

The voyageurs were sitting around the supper fire, drinking tea with extra sugar. "Energy liquid for the young," Louie called it. To this point there had not been much conversation in the evenings—three of them were just too tired. But on this night, which marked their first week away, Louie made a little speech.

"My children," he began quite formally, "I am proud of each of you. I cannot yet say that you are not pork eaters." The boys laughed, but Della had forgotten what the old term meant.

"We have only begun this ancient route of our ancestors. It will lead us many weeks into the west. We are sure to meet others traveling in the old style, as we have already done.

"I ask that you look hard and long at the places beside these waterways. They will not forever be as they are today. They were not always as you see them now. Take these places and our time together inside your hearts. There they will never change."

Louie's speech that night had been in French. Della knew he had not forgotten that they were going to speak English. She also knew, or supposed, that in their weariness, this was no time to start the boys on another voyage of the mind: English.

By the Mattawa River, all the body kinks were fading and they could talk or sing while paddling, which they certainly couldn't do while carrying their canoe and provisions over the numerous portage segments. Finally, on Lake Nipissing, Della asked in English, "How old will you boys be when your birthday comes one month from today?"

She was at her permanent position, milieux, or mid-canoe, and she turned back to look at Bobby, who was taking his turn as steersman.

"English, please," she said looking now from Bobby to Johnny.

The boys looked at each other, seeming to work their two minds as one. "Thirteen!" they finally shouted together in English.

"Yes!" Della squealed as loudly. Then she leaned over to kiss her paddle partner.

"Oy! None of that in my canoe!" roared their father. "Do you wish to throw us all into the lake?"

That night they did end up in the lake, clothes and all.

"Oh, Papa! You brought soap! I didn't even think of it!"

"We may be voyageurs, *ma petite*, but we are not savages!" He lathered his own whisker-grown face, then walked to the small mirror hanging on a tree to scrape at his beard.

Della grabbed the soap and ran into the cold water. First she rubbed it under her arms, and then walked out deep enough to do some other places. Finally, after she had worked a bit on her blouse and pantaloons, she ducked completely under the water and swished her long hair around and around. When she came up, she rubbed the soap over and over her head and scrubbed until her scalp tingled.

"It is not possible to keep the smoke out of your hair, Della," Johnny told her later. "You must have heard the women say that smoke follows beauty."

"Why, thank you very much, François John. If you will repeat that in English, I will tell you a bedtime story, just as I used to do when you were small."

She tied the large handkerchief that Gramma Nell had given her as a parting gift around her bushy hair and sat down on her blanket-rolled-into-a-seat.

Della began: "A long time ago in a land far away..."

"Red River it must be!" Bobby yelled.

"Shh! Quiet," Johnny said.

"No. No, I've changed my mind," their sister said.

"Oh, please Della," the boys said together.

"I won't—break in to you again," Bobby sputtered in English.

"Interrupt," Della said. "That's all right. Only I've decided to tell you another story instead. This one I heard from Mr. Hopkins on a winter's night that was as cold as this summer one is warm. And one that had a *lot* fewer insects! Why is it that Mrs. Hopkins never shows all these irritating little monsters in her beautiful pictures?" Della flapped her empty cup around her head, but managed only to stir the bugs' flight.

The twins nodded in unison. They handed her the container of bear grease which she rubbed on her clean face. The boys were serious now.

"All right. This story happened a long time ago too. But it is more like a legend. That means that it might actually be a true story."

"Was the—next—story not being true, Della?" Johnny asked.

"Well, that story—the *other* story—was a fable. Maybe we will try one of those *next* time."

Their father raised his eyebrows, shook his head, and placed two more pieces of wood on the little fire. Della began:

Madeleine was her name. Yes, a good French name. I'm not sure when she lived, but it must have been after the company began working this area. I mean, the region we left a week ago.

Her father completed his nightly chore of re-gumming their canoe and lay back with his head against a fallen tree. He was still smiling. But both boys were now closely following the slowly spoken English words.

Madeleine, who was maybe about your age, was working on her father's farm when there came an attack by Iroquois. Her parents were not there, but she knew what to do: Run to the fort! But in that place of safety were only two men and some young boys.

"Do you understand, brothers? Can you see Madeleine helping the little boys close the heavy gate? The door?"

The boys nodded again.

Well, now. There was a big problem because there were many Iroquois outside the fort and only a handful of French people inside and some of them were only little children. What could they do? Since the warriors did not attack the fort right away, that could mean that they did not know there were only two real soldiers inside.

That is what Madeleine thought to herself. So she and the two men and the little boys fired guns from many different places inside the walls. And they made a lot of noise by banging on the cook pots and by shouting.

Della reached forward with her metal cup and tapped it on their water kettle.

This shooting and noise from inside the walls went on for several days—maybe for two or three days. At last help came from Montreal and they were all rescued—saved from the Iroquois attack. And Madeleine is said to be a hero because she was so brave and clever—smart.

The boys put their heads together and began whispering in French. Della said sadly to her father, "Perhaps I should have just told them that Mr. Hopkins once had a very big black dog which he named Madeleine because she was so brave."

"We like to have a question, sister," Bobby said.

"Oh, yes. Of course." Della smiled happily.

"He carries a Scotland name, but Papa is mostly a Frenchman. Our mama is mostly an Iroquois," Johnny said.

"And you, sister, are mostly an English lady. But not when you come out here and wear trousers with us," Bobby added with a grin.

"Yes, all that may be true, but…" She did not continue.

"You have made us a problem. Not to know if we should like this Madeleine girl or no. Maybe it would be happier if Mama's Iroquois people kill the Frenchmens. But then, sister, that would be they are killing Papa's people." The twins ended their shared problem and looked worriedly at their sister.

"Time for sleep," Louie said, rising from his log. "We can try to solve all this another day. Maybe."

XVIII

Pots, Pans, and Porcupines

Into Lake Huron, across Georgian Bay, through Sault Ste Marie on both sides of the water. The boys were very strong and Della was becoming more so. The blisters on her hands had been soothed with bear grease, which also was used in the evenings to keep the mosquitoes from their skin.

"I like your hair in the plaits," Bobby told Della. "It makes me remember Mama."

"You will miss her," Della consoled. "I think of my mama, too, when I make braids. Not because Mama wore them herself, but because she always sang when she made them with my hair."

"A song! A song!" Big Louie shouted. "Who is our *chanteur* on this Brigade? Don't you know the song leader gets paid more than the ordinary milieux?" And Louie himself began the oldest of voyageur songs: *"Alouette, gentille alouette..."*

Every morning they ate a sort of breakfast, but only after the sun was well up and they had paddled many miles. Louie insisted on both, for safety. "You can feel for yourselves that there is less wind early in the daylight. We must take advantage of that for the times when we find the strong wind and it drives us into shore." More tea with sugar and a little boiled grain or dried fruit for energy was a must, they all knew. Their father had become especially fond of pemmican during his years

111

in the trade, so they chewed the pounded dried meat–berry–animal fat mixture mid-morning and mid-afternoon as they paddled.

Della found the traditional native travel food coarse and bitter, but welcomed it, as long as she had plenty of water to rinse her mouth. However, she didn't always swallow as much water as her brothers did, for they had a much more convenient way to let it out later on than she did.

There was no need for them to live off the land or even to carry many provisions with them. Louie and his crews had never done that in earlier days either. In the early days they simply did not have time to fish or hunt, though occasionally, usually by chance, some small animal would "hop into the pot." By the summer of the Macleod outing in the mid-1860s many of the original HBC trading posts had become the hub of small villages. The handsome *avant* was well known at each post and his coin and children were welcomed everywhere. While peas or corn or bean soup was still Louie's favorite fare, he purchased bacon and even eggs for his young ones.

After the first strenuous days had passed, Della found that she was able to do as her father suggested and allow the beauty of the land into her heart. She saw the reflections, which up to this time she had only noticed in Mrs. Hopkins' paintings. When they returned their canoe to the water before sun-up, she saw the mists that often engulfed everything. Della had wondered why Mrs. Hopkins didn't show things clearly, but now understood that the artist was painting realistically, even if such dense lake mists were difficult to believe.

She had expected to see animals every day, but often saw none at all. "Two hundred years of constant encounter with our men has not let so many of them escape," Louie told her. "When we reach the valley—maybe then."

They did not have to wait that long. Della almost stumbled over a huge porcupine on a "necessary" trip into the shadowy woods.

"Papa!" she screamed. She knew what the animal was, but not what she should do.

"Stand still, Della." It was Johnny who spoke. The animal had fanned its yellow quills high into the air. It also was standing still, but making threatening sounds.

Suddenly, *whamp!* A heavy limb struck the creature's head. The girl turned away so as not to witness all that came next. "You have found our supper, sister. Thank you very much." She heard the twins laughing.

It was, in fact, a welcome change to have chunks of roasted fresh meat in the stew of corn and peas. They all ate too much and sat long beside the dying fire. Bobby and Johnny were cleaning and sorting the quills and placing them carefully in a piece of soft leather. "*Our* trade items," they told her proudly. "We think there will be a pretty girl at Red River who will want to make earbobs of this old fella."

Della wondered if their language lessons were progressing *too* well.

Bobby returned from washing his hands in the river to say, "Tonight is your turn, Papa. Tell us about the early men—'A long time ago and far, far away...'" he began very solemnly, until breaking up with laughter.

Della playfully hit his shoulder with her fist. "Don't you want any more Aesop's Fables?" she asked sweetly.

Their father stretched back from the fire, rubbing his stomach. "Do you think you ate eight pounds of meat tonight, young ones?"

The boys smiled at him. "Perhaps eight *pieces* of meat," Johnny said. "No one could eat eight *pounds*."

"Oh, yes," Louie said. "Could and did. Many times. In a full day's time, that is." They knew the story was about to begin.

This was back in the days of one of the best men to ever enter the western trade, name of David Thompson. My mother's uncle traveled back and forth over the Rocky Mountains with him while he was trying, on and off, to find the upper Columbia River. Of course, in those days Mr. Thompson was with the Nor'westers, though he served back and forth a few times with the company, too.

"Papa? Do I remember his name from when I was a very little girl and you took me to the cemetery in Montreal to honor him? Can it be the same Mr. Thompson?" Della asked.

"You have an excellent memory, *ma petite*. You could not have been ten years old when he died. And you remember?"

"I think I only remember that you were saying goodbye to someone you cared much for," Della said softly.

"That I did," her father said as softly. "He *was* a man! A *coeur de bois* even though he came from England. But, young ones, he is not tonight's story—only that he is in it."

So, in their travels, always trading for pelts, my uncle and his men often went hungry, as did their leader, Mr. Thompson, too. And I do not mean, my sons, a little hungry, as you are when you say you are starving. They *were* starving!

He flung an arm around the neck of each boy and squeezed.

These men who actually *could* eat eight pounds of animal flesh a day, when it was available, would eat anything when it was not. Anything! Rotten meat, moss, mountain lion, all types of birds. Anything! By the pound! And sometimes what they ate would make them very, very sick.

But so it was. Sometimes they must even eat their dogs or horses. Which is what happened in this story, which Uncle Rene swore to be the truth. And, Uncle said there was proof of the event in the little notetaking book which Mr. Thompson kept to write what happened every day. Uncle Rene saw him write it there.

Louie broke a bit of brown sugar into each tin cup and poured them full again of deep black tea. Oh, he loved to tell this story!

Well, it seems that somewhere in those torturous Rocky Mountains (which I have crossed a time or two myself with the governor—the old governor, but by then we knew exactly where we were going, thanks to Mr. Thompson). Somewhere those early explorers had to eat a dog, which they all did. This time only one man became sick, and that didn't happen until several days later.

His name has come to us as Beaulieu and our countryman was in pain and like dying nearly two weeks without ever a stop. He could do nothing and nothing could his friends do for him. When finally their leader was called to the man for what might be the last time, Beaulieu placed the hand of his boss on the swelling of his left side and had Mr. Thompson rub it across lightly. There was a small, sharp object coming out from the center of the swelling in his stomach.

This was the apex of the story, so Big Louie paused and looked long into the fire-lit eyes of each of his children. They remained silent, as though holding their breath.

As with all great leaders of the trade, Mr. Thompson had some little amount of medical knowledge, plus a good deal of experience. He saw that the answer to his man's distress might come by removing a splinter from just under his left rib area. Slowly, Mr. Thompson drew out the object. And drew it out. And drew it out some more. The good leader must have wondered how any worker could wound himself so severely and not remember doing so.

But *no*! This was not a splinter of wood coming out of the man's stomach. It was a thick quill from the tail of a porcupine!

There was a sigh from three amazed listeners. "But, Papa," Johnny said. "*We* ate the porcupine, not Mr. Thompson's men. Is that not so?"

"Very true, my son, very true. However, Uncle Rene always said that, had Beaulieu eaten his portion of the dog they had shared ten days earlier like a *man* instead of like a wolf, he might have noticed that there was a porcupine quill in the dog meat and not taken it into his stomach—and then out the side of his stomach! Are you not glad, my sons, that your sister has become such a careful cook for *our* brigade?"

XIX

Seeing Red

And so they went: Lake Superior, with only one tremendous thunderstorm to slow their progress, and Grand Portage, the longest of hikes they would need to make on this old route. Here Della brought out her heavy shoes and made two carries with her share of their provisions and gear.

She had thought they would make two entire trips between Grand Portage, on the south side of the international border, and Fort Charlotte, on the Pigeon River, which formed that boundary line itself. But in this assumption she was mistaken. "I allowed you to rest two days at the American side so as to store up energy for the Grand Portage," Louie told them. "Not that we who were the originators of this trail ever had such time to spare, I can tell you truly." And so they had divided their equipment and followed Papa's directions.

"Because our canoe is a small one, I and one boy will carry it upright with a few objects inside. You other two will start off with a decent load of gear, walk a half mile—or, shall we say a quarter hour—and then set down that load and rest. Come back for one more load, take it to where you left the first load, set it down and rest. And continue thus until you have covered the eight-and-one-half miles. You boys will change off with me on the canoe. Della, *ma petite,* can you do it?"

As long as she didn't think of the Della who had worn a black pleated dress with sparkling white cuffs and collar at Saint Anne School or the Della who had spent long winters sewing by a cheerful fireplace or rocking precious babies, she thought she could.

On and on they traveled, using the routes long followed by the fur traders, first those from North America itself, then from France, then England and Scotland and Orkney, then the Americans, with many, many other nationalities thrown in as well. "Shoe and canoe, shoe and canoe," sang the boys through the maze of water and land called Rainy Lake and into small but treacherous Lake of the Woods, and then through the wild rice plants along the Winnipeg. At last they were paddling against the current of the north-flowing Red River.

"When will we reach the town, Papa?" Della asked.

"The town, petite? Which town do you speak of?"

"Why, Papa, Red River, of course."

"Then, my daughter, we have arrived! For the entire valley of this river is called Red River. There are farms and houses and stores and churches, and our people from the American border to Lake Winnipeg. And, for the first time since I was the age of these boys, I will not have to turn my *canot du Nord* around at once and start back to the east. Hurrah! Now we begin to live free!"

There was much about the next weeks that Della did not understand. Coming out of the English society in Montreal into the voyageur life of the wilderness was easier than coming from the wilderness into the Red River settlements. When she looked back on the experience in later years, she realized that she had sensed, but not recognized, the tension in the valley from the very beginning of her time there.

Big Louie himself seemed more lost in this region than ever he could have become along the trade routes. But the boys were delighted to be where there was activity more than of their own making. Also (though she told herself firmly that it must be only her imagination), her menfolk—every one of them—seemed not so willing to be in her company now.

"Cousins" her father had talked about during their trip seemed to materialize everyplace they stopped. The men—yes, she thought of the twins as men now—still slept outside or in outbuildings as they traveled up the river to Upper Fort Garry. But a spare bed, sometimes a separate room or an attic, sometimes even a blanket on the kitchen floor was found for Della. And she didn't mind returning to indoor, relatively insect-free comfort.

Louie seemed often to become immersed in deep political discussions with his male cousins—or maybe they were only French-speaking men he called his relatives. The boys easily found new friends their age who knew how to play some form of lacrosse. What surprised Della was that the girls here played the game, too.

Well, she told herself, she shouldn't have been surprised. These people had plenty of work about their farms to do, and from what she had heard the men saying, more than enough problems to make them want to lose their cares, when they could, in a lively game.

Della sat on the dried grass of a field behind their last stopping place before reaching Upper Fort Garry. She was watching Bobby and Johnny outmaneuver their host cousins in both stick and foot work. From the shade nearby she was catching sadness of voice as much as words such as "failed buffalo hunts," "scarce fish and game," and "drought, flood, and grasshopper infestations." Then came the most worrisome word: smallpox.

She rubbed her dirty hands down the legs of her now well-worn pantaloons and was about to get up for a little walk beside the river when a soft hand touched her shoulder. "Cousin Della. Tessa and I sometimes play too, if the boys will allow us. Would you like to?"

The word *no* almost slipped over her lips when Della saw that Cousin Annie would be ever-so-disappointed not to be involved with all those boys.

Annie and Tessa were the most interesting of the girls whom she had met thus far. Out here on the farm they also wore trousers that looked like they may have been hand-me-downs from their brothers. What Della didn't realize was that with her hair done up in braids and in her own blue pantaloons and moccasins, they thought she was about fifteen years old, too.

"Yes, all right. I will try," Della answered, and was rewarded with squeals.

She hadn't played lacrosse in years—not since several summers ago when she had visited her brothers across the river from Lachine. Ordinarily the stick and ball game was strictly for males, but, well, there was nothing ordinary about the Red River Valley.

The five boys made only requisite objections to three female players, and then consoled themselves. Maybe their game would be even more fun now that they had more players.

Up and down the dusty field they ran, sometimes forgetting who was on which team. They had only one big tree to use as a goal, so scoring was none too accurate, either; but none of this seemed to matter.

At the same moment that Della wondered what proper Mrs. Edward Hopkins would think to see her "dear" now, she took the wooden ball into her web from Johnny and cast it too far to the right of the tree and directly into the Red River of the North.

"Enough!" she shouted. "Enough! I'm going in after it. What about the rest of you?"

When they came dripping out of the cooling water, Della was met by her hostess, Cousin Ruth, who carried a drying cloth. "It has been arranged, Cousin Della. You will meet with Miss Wicks at her brother's kitchen for morning tea one week from today."

A week later no one would have recognized the trim little woman in the blue dress who toured the large fort at the confluence of the Assiniboine and Red rivers. Her hair was in a bun under a little straw bonnet (which she would surely alter a bit at first opportunity), and her feet were in shoes for the first time since making the Grand Portage.

Della's interview with Miss Susanna Wicks had gone well, and they were of the mutual opinion that the journey east in company should be a pleasure.

"My brother-in-law has arranged an escort," Miss Wicks had said. "But if you have worked for my friend Frances Hopkins, you will understand that an unmarried lady of *my* station *must* not travel unattended with a male. Why, what would people think?" Rolls of fat beneath Miss Wick's chin wobbled with her laughter.

Della rejoined Louie and a group of English and French men of mixed native and European ancestry—Metis, they were called here—outside the impressive Upper Fort Gate.

"...being attacked by the church, the government, *and* the company! What else can we do?" one of the strangers was saying, not so quietly. Big Louie saw Della and moved at once to offer his arm.

"Oh, Papa, I can wait with the boys. I found everything I needed and am in no hurry to leave this pretty place. Why, the chief factor's house is near as pretty as anything in Montreal, and certainly as big as some homes there. Why not enjoy your conversation a while longer?"

"No, *ma petite*. For today I have had enough of such talk. There will be time for that later."

Della was suddenly aware of the serious tone coming from this man who was nearly always so jovial.

"Papa," she said as they began to walk to the loaded canoe, "will you speak to me of all this before I must go east? I will need to know, won't I, before I leave my loved ones here?"

"Anyone with a new bonnet needs to know only one thing, daughter. And that is how very pretty she looks." He slipped her string bag of shopping over his shoulder and set off at a lively pace.

Their final stop together would be at Lower Fort Garry, a day's journey back toward the north. Louie tried to explain en route why two large posts of the same company had been built so near one another, but it was lost on Della. She had already begun to think of how few days she had left to be with her family.

On this part of the journey she was dressed like a lady, and she was feeling for the first time what Mrs. Hopkins must feel when she traveled: a passenger.

"…heard that there is someone in the area that may be quite a surprise to you when we get to the lower establishment. An "unexpected encounter," I think your poetry books might call it."

"What, Papa? I'm sorry. My mind had slipped quite far away. I'm afraid it was moving backward and forward in time at the same moment. What were you saying, Papa?"

"Nothing important, daughter. Only that, as I knew would be possible, we have found a proper lady to be traveling back to Montreal on your same schedule. Miss Susanna Wicks, sister to Mr. and Mrs. Johnson here at Lower Fort. She will be most happy to have an experienced maid and traveling companion."

"Yes, Papa. Miss Wicks is older—and larger—than I had expected. (Della extended her arms in a circle before her stomach), but I'm sure I can serve her satisfactorily."

The Lower Fort was more solid-looking, but not as inviting as the previous establishment. In any case, the Macleods' first lodgings would be about a quarter-mile distant in a camp for the local workers. There, accommodations would be more like those in the village Louie and the boys had left in Caughnawaga.

Della felt relieved to get back into her pantaloons and braids. The twins stowed their belongings in the guest tent issued them and literally ran off with their newly acquired lacrosse sticks.

Louie stood talking to a group of men not far away, but this time

Della made a point to hear nothing. She arranged their articles and took the colorful cotton fabric she had purchased in the Upper Fort from her string bag and began to rip and stitch. It felt good to be back at the handwork she was now so adept at doing.

Before the light was gone, she had four identical articles completed. And only four more days. Just four more, she thought. How could she leave her men here? Would it not have been easier to say goodbye from Gramma Nell's doorstep? She dried her eyes with her new going-home kerchief.

XX

A Sharp Game

Now there was only one day and one night left—a Sunday. Della was up and out into the river mist while her men slept soundly. They would not accompany her to mass, they had informed her. They would much rather sleep a few extra minutes in readiness for the big game.

"Of course the priests don't like us to play lacrosse on *their* day," Bobby had said. "Or the missionaries, either."

"Especially the missionaries," Johnny added.

"But then," Bobby continued, "what do any of them like about any of us?"

"They don't like that our people marry without any church blessing. They don't like that our people—and, I can tell you, some of theirs too!—wager on the outcome of the lacrosse games." This came from Johnny.

"And because the company doesn't like it, the church doesn't like that we—well, those of us who do—hold the best land in this valley." That came from Bobby. They still thought with one mind, even in English!

"It's all right, though, Della. The game will go on all day. You will have plenty of chance to see us play lacrosse this one last time."

This one last time, Della thought as she tied new kerchiefs around their necks once again. Then she said, "Papa. I have one for you, too. And one for my own hair." She could not look into Louie's misty eyes, but managed to finish her well-rehearsed little goodbye speech.

"Thank you, Papa, for this summer. I will truly never forget it. And I am going to ask Mrs. Hopkins to paint a picture of Canada just for me so that always, when I look at the picture or not, I will have the three of you near me." She had tied the blue print scarf around Louie's strong neck and her own around and under her heavy braids. This had been the perfect time to say goodbye, not tomorrow under the eye of Miss Wicks, whose "private escort" was coming to fetch her.

So as not to dirty her only traveling costume, Della changed after mass into pantaloons and moccasins before heading back toward the fort to observe the young men at play. Suddenly, there came Annie and Tessa at a run.

"Oh, Cousin Della. Isn't it exciting? Papa was so kind to bring us all this way just to see the competition between Upper and Lower. Have you ever seen so many handsome boys? Oh Della! Don't you wish we could be out there playing among them again?"

Della wished nothing of the sort. Already she was returning inwardly to her life as an English lady's maid. She did not thank Miss Wicks for causing the feeling, but knew the change was necessary. And she *would* be happy to make a much faster trip back to Gramma: a little way by river, a little by steamboat, a little by railroad, and there they would be right at Lachine station.

"Mama didn't come," Tessa told Della. "She said it was a crazy man's outing to see a wild man's sport. Mama says that when the young men get together like this, they are only playing at war. She doesn't like all the ancient ceremonies they do before they begin the game. Mama is very religious, you know."

There was a stony, open area outside the western wall of the Lower Fort. Whereas Upper Fort Garry was about half stone and half timber, Lower was totally surrounded by stone. Della thought this fort would have been established for military purposes, but, in fact, it was more an agricultural and storage-transport center.

Louie had assured his sons that they would easily find employment, possibly even a life-long trade at Lower. And, he had teased Della, large numbers of women also were employed by the company in the buildings and farm gardens. "You could certainly earn your keep as a day-laborer," he had told her. There existed here a gristmill for grains, a sawmill for nearby forests, and a brewery and a blacksmith shop, among a dozen other stone-built structures.

Today, however, the girls were interested only in the goings on *outside* the limestone walls: lacrosse. It was not easy to find a good viewing position because the ground was covered with sharp remnants of local rock that had been used to maintain the stone structures.

"It won't be too bad, even if we have to stand," offered Tessa. "Our brothers said that in this game they would be using the new rules suggested by that man in Montreal, Mister—what was his name, Annie, Mr. Bear?"

"No, silly," her sister said. "It was Dr. Beers! You can see there, the piles of limestone pieces the boys have set up to mark a field of play."

"If you are going to talk about silly," Tessa answered, "it is silly that there are going to be only twelve boys at a time playing for one team. What a waste when we could be looking over fifty or a hundred boys at once in a game. I don't think I am going to like Mister Dr. Beers' newly suggested rules!" Sometimes Della wished that she could find the opposite sex as interesting as these girls did.

The Sunday event had begun some time prior to their arrival. Many representatives from every cultural group were in the audience: French Metis and British Metis, Scots, Irish, English, and a handful of Americans. There were full blood North Americans from various nations, many bands of whom neither Della nor her companions could identify. And there were women, both older and younger than themselves.

At this gathering, too, shouts supporting one team or the other were mixed with whispers against a company who "nearly enslaved the native workers" and "was trying to steal our most valuable asset—land." Two words came up that Della had not previously heard mentioned: confederation and rebellion. She was not enjoying the contest as much as her brothers and her cousins were.

Finally! This was more interesting! Running across the field toward her little circle came both Bobby and Johnny. They had played together at this game so often that they moved nearly as one body. They were beautiful, she thought, with their black hair flying beneath the treasured identical kerchiefs tied around their sweaty foreheads. They were running and passing, and running directly toward her, when she heard a man call her name. "Della! Miss Della, is that you?" When she turned, there stood her old friend, Mr. Colin Steven, arm-in-arm with Miss Susanna Wicks.

It was hours before Della saw anything else. She woke to what sounded like a quarrel. "She will remain as long as need be," the woman's voice whispered firmly. "This is a company complex and she is my maid. I tell you, she will remain right in that bed!"

"Mrs. Hopkins?" Della whispered. "Are you home, Mrs. Hopkins? Am I home, too? Oh…" She slept again, but that may have been only for a short time. When she next awakened, she could see a little. Someone was holding her hand, but when she tried to turn her head, she could not, due to the pain.

"Papa—Papa, is that you?" There was a little chuckle, but it was not Big Louie's voice that answered.

"Welcome back to us, Della Macleod. If your other eye was not covered, you could see that it is not your big, strong father who sits with you now, only little Colin Steven, a man from your past."

Oh, her head hurt so! This must be a dream like she used to get when she had been a child.

"Is my papa here, Mr. Steven?" She felt sure she was crying, but felt the warmth of tears only on one cheek.

"He is coming back, miss. It will not be long." That was another man's voice, but not her father's. A weight was taken from the left side of her head; then, quickly, another weight was put in place of the first. The new one was very cold.

The second man said, "It is ice, young miss, from our icehouse. Lucky you are that we still had some few bits there in the straw."

"Oh," Della groaned. "What happened?"

Mr. Steven gently patted her hand. "It was an accident—or better said, a mishap caused by myself and your own athletic brothers, if they are who I suppose them to be."

"But what…?"

Not until the following day when she could sit up and sip the warm soup brought to her by a hovering Miss Wicks did Della learn the details. "Well, my young friend," the barrel of a woman said, "that nice Mr. Steven and I seem to be the root of your problem." For some reason Della felt Miss Wicks to be rather proud of her statement.

"You see, dearie," the woman continued, "when you turned to greet us, the boys played their strenuous ballgame—in what I understand is no longer the accepted fashion—right over top of you. Well, silly me. Of course that would never be the accepted fashion, but you understand what I *mean*. Then you went down on one of those sharp boundary stones and ended up here inside Lower's Big House attended by, not only the company doctor, but the two of us, who admit to our role in your destruction."

"I am so very sorry, Miss Wicks. If I understand you correctly, we have missed our departure to the east. This must make it very inconvenient for you."

"Oh, tut, girl. My time is my own and I could not want for a better escort in my delay—my new friend, Mr. Steven." She giggled like a girl. "Now, your family has gathered again. Shall I send them in?"

"Please do not kiss me, boys," Della pleaded. "And do not make me smile either," she added when they made sad faces.

"Sister, we are so sorry that our actions leave you here like this," Bobby began.

"Do you know that your whole forehead is put together with gum, like we would do to mend a birch bark canoe?" asked Johnny.

"And there was so much blood that Annie swooned and nearly fell on her own head."

"All right, boys," Louie intervened. "That's enough reporting for now. I'll meet you back at the Men's House shortly."

Big Louie spent his visiting time trying to convince his daughter to delay her departure until spring.

"Papa, I will mend as quickly along the journey back as I will lying here in this beautiful room. You and those boys have new lives to begin. And I feel sure that both Miss Wicks and Mr. Steven...you knew our old schoolmaster would be here, didn't you, Papa? Well, all three of us are expected in Montreal before winter."

The fort doctor agreed with Della, telling a doting voyageur father that yes, his girl was strong enough for the journey, and no, she would not be forever ugly. "You see, Louie, I was able to make most of the necessary stitches to her head in the eyebrow. I assure you that Miss Wicks has been instructed as to when and how those black stitches are to be removed."

The family finally parted a week following the planned Monday. Those eastbound would steam up the Red River into Minnesota. Not an uncomfortable route, Mr. Steven assured them. Then they would book modern transportation, both steam and rail, back to the St. Lawrence Valley.

XXI

Eyes and Ears

Miss Wicks was a tolerable travel companion and an excellent nurse. She changed the bandage every evening, replacing the soiled one with a soft cotton pad the company doctor had supplied.

"Now remember, Della, no matter how this irritates you with pain or itching or seeping, you are not to touch it or dislodge any of that ugly black—what is it anyhow—resin?" Miss Wicks said exactly the same thing with each new application. She also rubbed, ever-so-lightly, some of her own "miraculous" face creams into the purple-blue-yellow bruise below her patient's left eye. "Your bonnet almost hides the bandages, my dear, but *this* area is *so* unbecoming! And I have observed how young men look at you—until they see the discoloration."

Della had no concern about her appearance, but her head often ached, especially when their route included bumps of any nature. She dozed occasionally, but there was nothing in her recuperative naps to compare with Miss Wicks' habit of falling into a sound sleep mid-sentence.

"Do you think she is well?" Della asked Mr. Steven. "Or is it just the travel motion which makes her do so?"

Mr. Steven leaned close, but not too close, to Della's injured face. "I think, Miss Della, that her condition has more to do with the 'medicinal medications' she keeps in her little bottles than with any other cause."

"Oh my," Della said, embarrassed. Then she admitted, "I had wondered a time or two what the good lady drank from those little flasks."

She and Mr. Steven had opportunity for many enjoyable conversations. As soon as she was feeling well enough to talk and listen, Della asked how he had come to be in the Red River area to "cause," as he insisted he had done, her injury.

"That, young lady, is an extremely, *extremely* complicated secret."

"Oh, excuse me, Mr. Steven. I did not mean in any way to pry into your private affairs."

The man actually looked to see how near other travelers were sitting, glanced again at the softly snoring Miss Wicks, and began. "It will please and sadden me to share some of my thoughts with you, Della, as I have none other with whom I feel at liberty to speak. You have surely heard enough tales of the traveling man to understand what I mean by this."

Della nodded her head, then wished earnestly that she had not.

"Do you remember that I left Mr. Hopkins' employ rather suddenly?" he asked.

Della stopped another nod, and said yes instead. "We all missed you so very much, Millie and I particularly."

"Thank you, Della. I missed you girls, too. And the family setting, naturally. But, though I no longer worked for Mr. Hopkins privately, I was…perhaps it is clearest to say that I still received a salary through him—from the company accounts."

Della really did not follow this and her confusion must have shown on her face.

"As I said, the business is quite complicated. I will just continue on, as though to myself and hope that you can pick out some meaning."

It was not until years later and after many historic events had transpired that Della would remember his soft, burred voice and the information he had passed on to her so privately during their eastward passage.

Because this young man was an unknown who had never been involved in the fur trade business in any way whatever, and because he was a clever and resourceful man, Mr. Colin Steven had become unobtrusive eyes and ears for the HBC. He told Della that he had never done anything verging on the unethical, immoral, or illegal; he simply went places and saw and heard things. Except for his broad Scottish accent, he considered himself so ordinary as to be nearly invisible as, apparently, did others who talked openly around him.

He had learned that many American settlers to the west coveted the fertile lands of the Red River Valley. He heard rumors about American plans to annex that area to the Dakota territories.

He knew of a valley court case from about 1850 which resulted in a Metis man being found guilty, but because of the strong objection by hundreds of other Metis in the area, the man had not been punished for the crime. He had put this past history together with what he had been learning recently about Metis opposition to the HBC's continuing trade monopoly and was worried about implications on future operations.

Della had said, almost to herself, "Yes, I sensed the unrest very strongly while I was there. I felt, too, that there were motives unknown to me for my father's move into that area."

"I cannot help but have personal feelings about much of what I have learned," her friend had continued. "And nothing at all about what I observe is ever written down, therefore the reason for my many travels. If necessary, my presence can be explained as the forward man for expansion and diversification of trade in western Canada. Which, in all honesty, I am doing, but only in the interests of the HBC.

"It will not be far into the future when all company outposts will operate like that of Lower Fort Garry. Each post will be a storehouse for gathering and distributing local or imported goods. It's an exciting concept—one worthy of my travels, if nothing else were."

Mr. Steven was warming to his lesson, as he had used to do in the Hopkins' classroom. "Why, Della. Do you know there was a man back at Upper this trip who was talking about some company in—France, I think it was—yes, probably Paris. He said that the company there draws up pictures and makes a book which they call a business catalog of all the possible items that folks way out in the countryside could write back and ask for. Now, that's an idea I could even become interested in myself. Of course, you would have to be able to trust your postman not to run away with whatever it was you ordered."

"I don't mean to quiet our laughter, Mr. Steven," Della said after a short silence. "But you mentioned sad things, too. What can be so sad that the company would be interested to hear?"

"There! You have hit the point exactly! It seems to me—or I'd better say, to the people whose conversations I overhear or who I entice into conversation—that the company has been and will be interested in only one thing: profits! Yes, naturally the shareholders in London want a good return on the money they have invested. And, until recently, they have had nothing whatever about which to complain. But when the *honorable* company abducts little orphan children off the London streets and sends them here as so-called indentured servants, then they had better call it by the practice outlawed in Britain a hundred years ago—slavery!"

"Slavery? Slavery! What is this talk of slavery? That war has already been settled. It is land now—who owns the land and how much *land* is the company willing to give up—so that we here in the farther north do not end up in the same dreadful civil war situation!" Miss Wicks was, obviously, awake again. Della wondered how long she had been listening.

Della explained, "Our escort was telling me something of the troubles possibly approaching our friends in Red River."

"By 'our friends,' missy, are you referring to those of Mr. Steven or those of yourself?" the woman asked sharply.

Della shot back without thinking, "If the word *friend* is used, Miss Wicks, would we not have to be concerned for them all?"

Mr. Steven patted Della's hand to calm her while Miss Wicks became very busy with the cork of her little medicine bottle.

XXII

In a Fog

"What a wonderful friend you are, Emma," Della said from a foamy, deep tub in Gramma Nell's kitchen.

"Any child that goes wanderin' 'round the wilderness, then decides to take a bath in the middle of winter needs a friend," the black woman responded. "I check in on your grandma every day anyway, and today we've decided to help you with your bath."

Gramma Nell stood behind Della and tipped the girl's head back gently. "We're going to wash that hair until it squeaks!" the old woman announced. "Emma has two full buckets of hot water from the wash house and, my sweet, if you must be spotless for the reunion with Family Hopkins, we are the experts to make you so."

The women oohed and aahed at the purple scar forming above her left eye as they unwound Della's braids. "You pour that water, Emma. I'll do the scrubbin'. We promise not to hurt you any more than you've already done to yourself, girl." They all laughed.

A restful sleep in her own bed and a thorough scrubbing had revived Della to the point where she gladly shared her western adventures throughout the early November evenings in Lachine. Then it was time to return to the big house in Montreal—and a reunion with Millie. They would have so many things to talk about.

Della stood on the same platform where she and Gramma Nell

had awaited the same train carrying nearly the same family eight years earlier. She was now able to stand still without instruction, but she was just as excited.

At last, there they came: Mr. and Mrs. Hopkins, then Raymond, Wilfred, and Olive. Then…it was not Millie. Millie must be behind that older, dark-haired matron. But the next people to alight were businessmen, then another Lachine family.

The children were all around her now, hugging at her skirts, and Mr. Hopkins was seeing to their luggage, along with Izzy, Emma's husband, who had taken over Sim's job when the old man died.

"Della—Della, dear? Are you all right? You look so pale. And what is this you've done to your forehead?"

Mrs. Hopkins was speaking—greeting her, but Della barely heard. "Millie?" was all she could say.

"My dear. Didn't you receive her joyous letter? Millie was married—oh, months ago now. I'm sure she wrote to you. Yes, I remember her bubbling on, as only our Millie can do, about how pleased her friend Della would be for her."

It was several days before Della could appreciate how kindly she had been treated by Frances Hopkins. The children's new nanny had been assigned a small room adjoining the nursery-school room. Della had been engulfed by yards of fabric to be turned, posthaste, into holiday outfits for the much-grown children. Millie's letter had been "found" by Wally. Mr. Wall said he "…must have been so shocked at the sight of Della's face when she arrived back in the kitchen that he had forgotten to give it to her."

Della wavered during those first days between gladness for her dear friend's good fortune and self-pity that she had lost Millie just at the time when she was also without her father and the twins. She reread Millie's letter nearly every night.

Dear Dear Della,

I am a married woman! Oh, Della! I am so very happy!!! The only gray cloud is that you were not present to share my happiest hour. You are probably wondering how this all came about so speedily. Well, I can say that our marriage, and from this point, both of our lives, was and will be ruled by the sea.

Captain Scott (that handsome man I first met in a cemetery!) was awarded shore time only a few days after we H. Family arrived in June. Neither of our families (and certainly not Alan nor I) were opposed to our taking advantage of the opportunity presented to begin our life together, so we were married in St. Savior's Church, Paddington, on August 10th. Did you ever know that this is the church where Mr. and Mrs. H. were married? Can you believe this, Della? Mr. Edward & Mrs. Frances stood up with us! And even the children, who I will miss, but will replace with my own as soon as possible, were there for the marriage ceremony.

You must not fret that you and I will never see each other again. After all, I am now a Captain's wife! And certainly our letters will find their paths to each other _often_. Before I close (my _husband_ is patiently waiting) I wanted to include this bit of information so that you, dear friend, may look to your own future.

Mr. & Mrs. H. have purchased a home at Cumberland Place in Hyde Park where they will live as soon as the company allows him to retire. That can't be long now, Della, so I do hope you are making your own plans.

I love you and think of you often and miss you. You will hear from me again soon.

Your friend forever,
Millie _Scott_

∗ ∗ ∗

In the years following the marriage of her friend, Della had three means of keeping track of time's passage: constant growth of the children, necessitating new garments; infrequent messages from her family in the North West, generally only mentioning their good health; and an array of young men presented to her by Miss Nora LaFleur, who happened to know a great many young men.

Only one of these young friends attracted Della's interest, and she recognized the reason at once: he was a Norwegian.

"Mrs. Bakke, may I present the one who created your lovely new bonnet," Nora had said on a day in early spring. "This is Miss Della Macleod, my business associate. And this…" Nora turned to the tall golden man accompanying the older woman.

"This is my son, Bjørn Bakke. It is thanks to his generosity that I have the pleasure of this new bonnet," said Mrs. Bakke.

That had been their first meeting, and Della had held the memory of those few moments close in her heart for weeks afterward. She and Nora sometimes took tea together on a Wednesday afternoon when Della was free. They both recognized that an attempt at matchmaking was in progress, but this did not interfere with their association.

"Nora," Della began, on a day not long after meeting the mother and son. "Would you mind if I asked what you know about Mrs. Bakke and her son?"

"I would mind if you did not ask, eventually, you precious girl. And I suspect it is not the mother who you would like to learn about."

Della remained silent, though her cheeks flamed above her teacup.

"In any case, I know about *her* only that she is a recent widow, as you yourself could conclude from the black bonnet she purchased. Or, I should say, *he* purchased. The young man is the heir to a timber empire somewhere in the west—or is it the south? Are you interested, Della?"

138

How does one know if she is "interested"? And what did these new sensations in her body mean? They only happened when she thought of his red-gold hair and the even redder side whiskers. Maybe she had formed an image of Mr. Longfellow's saga-man years earlier and was trying to insert Mr. Bakke into that role. Maybe the passing years, Millie's happy marriage, and gentle hints from family and friends had been working on her.

"Because if you *are* interested, we will be seeing Mr. Bakke after church this coming Sunday."

Della's teacup rattled back into its saucer.

"Yes, *cheri*. He came into the shop—for no good reason, I can tell you—last week. I feel quite safe in assuming that he expected to find you there."

"Oh, Nora! You didn't say..."

"*Cheri*! Have I not played at this game enough myself to manage discretely? I mentioned simply that with the spring weather returning, it would be pleasant once again to walk along the riverbank with my young friend after mass on Sunday. In this way, you will both be made aware of the other's interest, but—gently, shall we say."

With Nora trailing at a distance and feigning interest in scenery and objects she had observed hundreds of times, the three walked several Sundays along the St. Lawrence. Mr. Bakke tipped his tall silk hat respectfully to each lady he approached and stopped a time or two to converse briefly with gentlemen. While Della was pleased enough to be seen in company with such a man, there was an awkwardness between them that was not eased by an afternoon at the first outdoor concert at the bandstand or a poetry reading sponsored by the municipal library.

During these several times together, she had learned only that his name meant "bear hill," that he had been born in Minnesota, and that he had an undefined number of sisters in undisclosed settlements along unnamed rivers. When Della had attempted to tell her young man the humorous story of Miss Wicks administering drams of brandy to them *both* before drawing the hardened old stitches from her eyebrow, Mr. *Bare* Hill (she could almost hear Millie calling him) had curled his lips, then hurried them along the park walkway.

There was a gentle pressure on her right shoulder and Della jumped with a start. "My dear, I've asked twice about the reading of Mr. Longfellow's poetry. Was it something Mr. Hopkins and I will be sorry to have missed?"

Della wondered how long she had stood staring out the studio window and what, exactly, it had been that Mrs. Hopkins had asked her to find.

"Oh, Mrs. Hopkins. How did you know when you had found the right man to marry?" It was an anguished question of a type seldom shared between these two. When Della sank down onto the little stool she had once used to pose for Minnehaha, Frances knew the time had come for a carefully worded answer.

The artist did not display her emotions often, nor did she readily share her thoughts with anyone save her husband. At the moment, however, this girl, who had become nearly as dear as one of her younger sisters, needed the wisdom of a woman.

"I believe, Della, that there must be an immediate friendship. At least in my own case and from what I have discovered from those in my family, that seems to be a very good indication. If a man and a woman can converse as friends—why, think of our good Queen Victoria and the wonderful friendship and love she shared with her Albert. Yes, communication and respect in a happy and comfortable manner must be the foundation for love and an enduring relationship."

Mrs. Hopkins turned suddenly away, realizing that she had seldom spoken in such a way with her hired staff, even Della. But on second thought, she turned back and asked softly, "Have you found someone special, Della dear?"

* * *

Miss Della's Bonnets had gained in popularity with Nora's clientele and Della welcomed the additional income. She insisted that Gramma Nell accept a part of that extra money. Though the old lady no longer worked in the big Lachine house, she had been allowed to remain in her cottage, as a sort of pension, but she had no other income.

Della still saw the Ross women in Lachine, and talked of when they had been maids together. She enjoyed with them, their husbands, and some other old friends from school a winter tobogganing party along the frozen St. Lawrence. Mrs. Hopkins also maintained her close friendship with the Sisters at Saint Anne's. On this winter afternoon, when Mrs. Hopkins had come by to fetch Della for their journey back to Montreal, the artist had been so taken by the group's activities that she had done an on-the-spot sketch of them all playing in the snow.

Visitors had always been plentiful at the Hopkins' homes. It was known that, not only did Mrs. Hopkins delight in entertaining, she prided herself on doing it especially well. Della became more and more a social secretary and assistant to her employer, a role that might have caused envy in other members of the household staff had the girl not been so loved.

As such entertainments increased, so did the number of new faces or new titles to remember. Lord and Lady Monch changed from being known as the governor general of British North America and his lady to the governor general of Canada and his lady. They were special friends of the Hopkins. Then there were military guests who advanced continually in rank and importance.

Mrs. Mildred Browne, the new nanny (in no way to be thought of as Millie's *replacement*!) did not approve of so much merrymaking. "It upsets the household, and therefore the children, to have strangers forever intruding," as she put it.

At tea one evening, the cook, Mrs. Roberts, reminded the complaining woman that, but for the kindness of Mrs. Hopkins taking a near-destitute, childless widow-friend of one of her sisters into that *upset* household, "...you, Mrs. Judgmental Browne, would be scrubbing floors in the big houses of London!"

Further complaint was not heard, but Della worried that Mrs. Browne lavished attention on Raymond and Wilfred at the expense of young Olive. With her mother's permission, Della would take little Olive along on her trips to Nora's shop. Not only did it give the child some special attention, but her company also diverted undesired advances by Nora's male friends. Della felt that Mrs. Hopkins was none-too-keen on her association with the notorious Miss LaFleur. However, she knew that Frances trusted in her caring regard for the child.

In a letter to Millie, congratulating her on the arrival of her second child, Della wrote:

> You would not believe the unrest I feel in these last years without you. So very much better do I understand now your desire to have your own life in your own land.
>
> Remember when I wrote about the tension I sensed during my summer in Red River? Millie! I am now feeling—and actually hearing talk of—similar difficulties right here in the East. Only now, after becoming more aware through comments made to me by our friend Mr. Steven, I worry more about the future of this land than I do about my own future.

Those concerns were displaced in early 1869 by one much nearer to home. Frances Hopkins had been delivered of her fourth son. As with each previous birth, the mother had recovered her vigor rapidly. This little baby never did become vigorous. Both Mrs. Browne and the doctor tried their best, but the child's health was too fragile. He died in infancy, leaving, for the second time, the family in grief at the loss of a child.

As she had done five years before, Frances attempted to ease her broken heart through painting. She paged back into her sketchbooks and turned those exhilarating experiences into big, bright, bold canvases.

"These will be my children now, Della, along with my memories. What do you think, Della. Will anyone want to buy Canadian scenery? Will anyone invest in a canvas this large?"

"I would invest, Mrs. Hopkins, if you would paint for me my father and his band of voyageurs paddling through the wilderness."

"It is natural to miss him, dear. I must not lose track of the fact that loss is not mine alone. Here, help me set this canvas on those two easels, and let us see what develops."

What developed were the talents of Frances Anne Hopkins. She painted as Della watched and encouraged. Day after day the oversized canvas grew with life. There were three canoes being paddled into the fog of Lake Superior. Only in the third craft could passengers and voyageurs be clearly seen, but Della knew from her own experience on that entrancing waterway that Mrs. Hopkins had captured her father's craft exactly.

There in the center of that last canoe sat Frances and her husband, he with his pipe, she with her book of poetry. Big Louie stood in the bow with his back to the viewer. (If only she could have seen her father's face!) His steersman, standing also, was more clearly visible. They guided their craft with the strength and calm that came from a lifetime in birch bark.

On the day *Canoes in a Fog* was completed, Frances startled Della by pulling her up from the studio workbench and hugging her soundly. "That, Della, will be my most famous child. I will offer it to the Royal Academy in London for summer exhibit. Now, what do you think? Will anyone there appreciate my artistic efforts?"

XXIII

Gift and Confusion

There came a gentle knock at Della's door the evening before the dress ball. This gala event would see Edward and Frances Hopkins away on what was to be one of their final crossings from Canada to England.

The maid, Nancy, announced softly, "Miss Della, the mister and missus would like to see you in his study." As such a summons was a rarity, Della descended the back stairs trying to think what could put her in such alarm.

The library fire was bright and both of her employers smiled as she entered, so Della was more at ease. "Good evening, Della." Frances began. She did not seem to know what to say next.

"We asked you in, Miss Della, to say a special thank you for the years you have been with us. Why, I remember," he said with a smile, "the winter you were born."

Noticing his wife's look he cleared his throat and began again, "Of all our staff, except for your grandmother (who we still regard as ours), you have been with us the longest. Naturally, you are aware of the changes coming. But tonight we…" Della saw Mrs. Hopkins take something up from the settee on which she was seated, "…we have a gift in appreciation of your loyal service. My dear wife says it is something you, above all people, will appreciate."

Now it was Mrs. Hopkins' turn. "Possibly you were a little disappointed when you suggested a picture of your father and I came out with him in a fog." Mrs. Hopkins chuckled a little at herself. "It's all right, Della. I understood your emotion. So right then I began another picture in—shall I say, in private."

Mrs. Hopkins held up a large, framed watercolor. A stately birch bark canoe showed very clearly her father seated in the bow wearing a hat with his trademark feather, and a water lily tucked into the band. His steersman, clearly Simon de Lorme, stood before the HBC British ensign fluttering from the stern. Della could recognize the faces of each of the voyageurs and wondered how Mrs. Hopkins had captured them so accurately.

In the center of the canoe, as she so liked to do, Mrs. Hopkins had included herself dressed in a blue, net-draped hat that Della had fashioned for her to help keep off the mosquitoes. Beside this little blond lady sat a bearded Mr. Edward Hopkins, holding his long-stemmed meerschaum clay pipe and wearing his beaver-felt travel hat. There were water lilies and rocks and reflections. Behind all this was a rock cliff and a waterfall. It *was* Canada.

Della rubbed at the pinkish-white scar above her left eyebrow, as she often did now when she was emotional. She was on the verge of tears and did not trust her voice, even to say thank you.

"Here, Della. Please sit down. Here, beside the fire." Mr. Hopkins guided her to a chair.

Mrs. Hopkins continued, "You see, my dear, this picture, which I must tell you, I have plans to enlarge and reproduce in oils, is not just for service past." Frances seemed to nod to her husband to continue.

"While we are retiring soon, the details are not yet complete. In fact, there are matters…ah…numerous…ah…conflicts to be taken into consideration before my position with the company is concluded."

Frances took up their obviously rehearsed presentation. "We wish to hold the residence here in Montreal for a bit longer. But as we will take Mr. Wall, Mrs. Browne, and the children with us to our new home in London, we wish to ask that you and Mrs. Roberts keep things together here, for a bit longer. Are you willing to continue on with us so indefinitely, Della?"

Della was finally able to say, "You honor me with both your gift and your request."

✻ ✻ ✻

It was not at all difficult to "keep things together" in Montreal. With only the two women in the big house, very little needed to be done except to eat and to dust occasionally. But, as in every prior period when the family had been absent, the house was simply too silent to keep Della inside it.

She visited Miss Nora's, as the shop was called, on a regular basis and always enjoyed Nora's outspoken conversation. There was a very small living space behind a curtain at the rear of the shop. It held Nora's bed, a small table, a little round stove, two chairs, and two rockers. This became their chat and work room when no customers were at hand.

Nora did most of the chatting and Della the listening, mainly because it was her habit to use her mouth to hold various adornments for her bonnets. Nora seemed never to run dry of topics to talk about.

On an afternoon in early March 1870, Della was alone in her rocker when Nora flipped back the dividing drape and said determinedly, "We must get out of here for a few hours, my pet. If I listen to one more wealthy, spoiled matron giving me her version of politics—actually, I believe that last was her husband's version, but coming out of *her* mouth…I swear, Della! I sometimes have to restrain myself from running my pins through something other than the fabric!"

It was very cold, but not windy, so Della suggested timidly that they walk over to the Mercantile Building and view the Sixth Exhibition of the Art Association of Montreal. "Mrs. Hopkins has submitted quite a number of color sketches for display. It might be nice to let our eyes view something at a little distance for a bit."

Surprisingly, Nora was all for the idea. "It will be good to be seen in such a cultured setting. Good for business, that is," Nora said. They placed dark, warm bonnets on their heads and wrapped themselves in wools and fur muffs. Then, turning the sign in the window so that it read *Please Come Back Tomorrow*, they set off.

Of course, Della already knew which of Mrs. Hopkins' pictures would be on display. If she remembered correctly, there would be sixteen in number. Each was a picture of Canada: a riverside camp, voyageurs in and out of canoes, rivers and landscapes, native boatmen. Nora gave the works of her former employer careful attention. In fact, she studied several of them intently. Then they moved along to view others' work.

During their return to the shop, Della could not resist the question, "What did you think of her work, Miss Nora?"

"And why should you ask me, Della? My artistic interests do not lead me in *that* direction. I will say this, though: seeing churches and sailor boys and a stream in Wales or a town in Switzerland—what the *other* artists offered was more worth my ten cents' admission than seeing a way of life any person in this area has seen for the past—it must be two hundred years. Are such scenes really what a *lady* should be spending her talent on?"

Della wanted very much to defend Mrs. Hopkins' entries in the exhibit. She wanted to tell Nora—and some of the other Exhibition viewers whom she had overheard muttering similar sentiments about the pictures—that a record of local life was *exactly* what Frances had intended. She wanted to tell them all that someday they might be glad that someone, other than Mr. Notman with his colorless photographs, had preserved a way of life that was already being replaced by "progress."

Della remained silent, however, out of a desire to continue the good relationship she had with her so-called business partner. Never would she mention any of the overheard comments to Mrs. Hopkins. Never!

⋆ ⋆ ⋆

Edward and Frances had returned from England aboard the *Prussian* in late January. Shortly afterward Della had assisted in readying the art display to which she would later invite Miss Nora. Mrs. Hopkins had seemed somewhat agitated by a "lack of foundation material" as she had put it.

Della, always ready to soothe, reminded her that she had, in addition to the work that would soon be displayed, several other sketchbooks from last year's tour of inspection when she had been with her husband as far west as Thunder Bay in Lake Superior. "But, Della, don't you understand, dear? I must have enough from this area to last a lifetime. A lifetime!"

The house was not silent that early summer of 1870. It was not children's running feet that filled it, but military boots. Della had served tea to Mr. Hopkins and his uniformed guests—were their names Young and Lindsay? Another time Sir Stanfford Northcote visited. On this occasion in April, she and Mrs. Roberts had been closely supervised by Mrs. Hopkins herself because Sir Stanfford Northcote was governor of the esteemed HBC so everything had to be perfect. Edward was only weeks from the end of his successful career with the company and this caused Frances to be even more determined that this guest *must* receive an unforgettable welcome.

Not unexpectedly, the event was memorable—for the governor would write of his visit in his journal, saying that he had seen his hostess' drawings of the 1869 inspection tour and had found them "very interesting."

Somehow, without any actual explanation, Della had come to

understand (possibly by her quick mind piecing together snatches of conversation with just such visitors) that Mr. Hopkins was to guide some sort of military expedition to the west—to Red River—later that summer.

Words such as "unrest" and "resistance" were floating about Mr. Hopkins' library, along with the leather, wool, and tobacco smells of the military. As she had done all her life when she encountered similar tangles, Della tried to make sense of the situation by talking with her grandmother.

"It's not an inconvenience, Gramma Nell. I may visit nearly as often as I wish now that there are no children about. And today there are no guests to be tended. I need only return in time to help Mrs. Roberts with the evening meal."

Some months back Nell had asked Izzy and Emma to move her bed into the cottage main room nearer the fire. She was spending more and more time in bed, as the years wore on. "But, sweet one, my Della, you know your little cot is right there in my old room whenever you can find the time to use it."

"I know, Gramma. But I am happy just to talk with you like this. You always know so much for one who gets out so little."

"I don't have to 'get out,' Della. You know that," Gramma teased. "Why take this big body anyplace when all I have to do is open that door to friends." And the girl knew it was true. "Now, Della. Tell me what it is that worries you."

It was a good thing that Della no longer had her normal chores to do, because the telling took most of the afternoon. "I have tried to remember my history lessons from the good Sisters, Gramma. It just seems so long ago and so confusing. Upper Canada and Lower Canada; the Maritimes and Rupert's Land—which belonged to the company and covered more territory than all the other places put together." Della sighed, but Nell remained silent, knowing that the

149

girl would remedy her troubled mind in her own way.

"You remember how much I learned about what the Sisters would probably call 'our culture' when Papa took me to Red River. Well, that area seems to be mentioned more and more often. I am worried about all this preparation for what is being called the Red River Expedition. Anyone can see that it is definitely military in nature."

Della was sitting on the edge of Nell's bed and reached out now for her grandmother's cold hand. "I know my papa well. He has always been a man of strong convictions. And I fear that his sons are very like him in that way. The boys are sixteen now. Can you believe that, Gramma? They are French Canadians living in an area desired by people who are not. I am meaning both British and American farmers who covet the land along the Red River.

"Oh, Gramma. I try to understand what I read in the *Gazette* about surveys and land titles and Mr. Bruce and Mr. Riel—who are both being called rebels. But, I think it is possible that many of the printed stories get—well, maybe they get mixed up by the time they have traveled all that distance between Red River and here."

Della realized that she was nearly wringing her grandmother's hand, so she let go and, with a big breath said, "The churches have become involved; the French want to speak French and the British want only English spoken. Oh, Gramma, it's so confusing and worrisome. And all the time I think of the boys and Papa out there."

"Yes, child, yes. Even here in this room I have heard much about this trouble. And I have come to the same conclusion: it is confusing beyond belief. But now that we are united into the Dominion of Canada we have to hope that *all* those who are in control will be sensible."

XXIV

Ladies All Together

One person was not being at all sensible about the situation: Frances Anne Hopkins. In her quiet way she had talked and explained and pleaded, until finally she had convinced Edward to allow her to travel along with the army expedition he was to escort through company lands. Her winning argument may have been, "But husband, I have been informed that there *will* be a European lady along. Her name is said to be Kate St. John and she is the wife of the news correspondent from the Toronto *Globe*. Surely with my experience…"

The artist had become terrifically excited about the prospects of spending more time in the North West. "Or," she asked Della, "should I be calling it Manitoba? It is a good thing I am a painter and not a verbal historian!"

As part of her preparations, Mrs. Hopkins asked Mrs. Roberts to serve afternoon tea to her and Della—and a guest. "Della, this is my new friend, Lady Louisa Wolseley. Mrs. Wolseley, my assistant and friend, Miss Della Macleod. We have been discussing our first impressions of Canada, Della." And, by way of including the girl in their conversation, she asked, "Did you ever know that my interest began in Scotland?"

Della knew little of the early life of this fine lady who had become her friend. "In Scotland, Mrs. Hopkins?" she said, somewhat surprised. "I've not heard you speak of being there."

"Oh, please, Mrs. Hopkins," said Lady Wolseley. "Do tell. You have heard my account of my husband's military exploits and of mine in becoming a mother for the first time. Let us hear about you."

Della would not have been surprised had Frances declined the request, so private was she about her personal life. But this guest was very special and the situation was unusual.

"We were five little girls," Mrs. Hopkins began, "on a voyage of exploration with our father. I think, now that I have a large family of my own, how brave my parents were to take us all on board ship to the Islands of Orkney that summer. But, as you know Lady Wolseley, military men lead where *they* choose to go."

"How very true. Do go on," the honored guest encouraged.

"Actually, I remember very little and possibly that is as it should be, because we three older girls, along with our governess, became separated from the family. I do remember an old gentleman sitting dockside. He suggested that we, 'the lost' he called us, should sit down and wait to become 'the found.' Meanwhile, he told us stories of his birthplace—Canada, he called it. Although an island in the Arctic regions of this vast land had been named for my father, I'm sure it was my first hearing of the word Canada. I didn't forget it—nor will I ever."

There was a long silence. The two older ladies exchanged a glance.

"By way of getting to know you, Miss Macleod," offered Lady Wolseley, "would you tell me something of the Red River area? I understand that you have traveled there by canoe."

Della was at a loss as to how she might answer. She and Mrs. Hopkins had sometimes discussed this or that about their common experiences along canoe routes in the wilderness, but Della's journey had been very different from that of the privileged wife of a company officer. And—she had *never* spoken to any other Hopkins' guest about herself. That simply was not done!

In addition, her agile mind was flicking of its own accord to females in trousers, strong-smelling little flasks, and the north-flowing Red River. But, yes! There she had it!

"Would you mind, my lady. I have a story, but it is not mine. I have heard my father tell it—about his people, the voyageurs. My retelling it now might acquaint you with the land and the people, and at the same time introduce you to the Red River Valley."

"Oh, yes, please," said both ladies at once, and Della noticed a very delighted look from Mrs. Hopkins.

"The story is not so very old, possibly only twenty-five years. It began at the Storehouse near where we lived in Lachine." Della composed herself.

"You will see the place shortly," Frances murmured to Lady Wolseley.

This is a religious story—no, more correctly, a story about religion. And it is indicative of the flowing together which occurs in our land. I remember the major character because he had such an unusual name: George Jehosaphat Mountain. He was bishop of the Anglican Church and visited St. Stephen's Anglican located just behind my school in Lachine.

Old Governor George Simpson, who was a member of Saint Stephen's congregation, was asked to provide a *canot de maitre*—a big Montreal canoe—to transport this bishop between Lachine and Red River where he would—oh, I suppose he was going to determine what should be done about churches there.

"Now, ladies, the reason for my father's telling this story is that his father, my *grandpere*, was involved." She continued more confidently. "Governor Simpson hand-picked the voyageurs who were to transport such an important personage. There were eight French Canadians and six Iroquois from Caughnawaga. They were, every one of them, Roman Catholics.

"The North American People's village has a beautiful little church across the river," Frances whispered to her guest.

My *grandpere* was not avant, or first in the canoe, as my father would later become. Grandfather was steersman, or last and there he stood the entire thousand and more miles to Red River—stood when he was not helping to haul baggage for the Bishop and his chaplain and his personal servant around the rapids and waterfalls of the western trade routes. But this, ladies, is only the background for the story. After traveling for thirty-eight days in the way I have described, these seventeen men in their huge canoe at last entered the waters of Lake Winnipeg. This they did on a Saturday evening—an important detail in the story because the bishop, as we might all understand, had his heart set on being at the Lower Red River Church for the Sunday morning services. The guide conferred with his voyageurs. The bishop (I presume) said his prayers, and it was agreed that the paddlers would continue their strenuous work throughout the night in an attempt to reach their destination in time to please God and the bishop. Yes, I will tell you now, even before the end of my story, that they *did* accomplish their goal. But you must imagine them doing so by paddling through torrents of rain and in dark so complete that had their guide, a veteran my father called Uncle Jacques, not known the landscape by *feel*, they might have missed the mouth of the Red River where it flows into Lake Winnipeg. These brave and strong Canadians had traveled nearly a full twenty-four-hour day to reach their resting place. And what do you suppose they did in celebration at the end of so much paddling?

At this point Della stopped, amazed at her own emotional involvement in a story she had heard so many times. She looked from Mrs. Hopkins to Lady Wolseley. "My dear ladies, they sang as though they were as fresh as that Sunday morning. They sang!"

The exchange of stories was, in fact, the last easy thing about the women's Red River Expedition. Louisa Wolseley, who had been married only a little more than two years to the Royal Army Officer who would lead the expedition, came to like and trust this dark-haired

French Canadian girl immediately. Though there were many, many details to be worked out in rather a short period of time, Frances Hopkins was sure all could be arranged. Their first session together had ended on a very positive note with Lady Wolseley saying in a confidential way, "We may never see the *other* European lady who will be going along with her husband—I believe he is a newspaper man—but I can't imagine that anyone in this mixed and motley group will be in such good company as the *three* of us."

It happened then that these women, somewhere in the mass of about 750 British Regulars and Canadian militiamen, and a like number of white and Indian voyageurs traveled west along approximately the same course that the Macleod Brigade had followed some years earlier. It was a noisy, colorful, exciting and successful expedition, when lack-of-bloodshed under difficult conditions is considered.

Lady Wolseley was rightfully proud of her already distinguished husband's leadership. Not only had he managed the logistics of transporting hundreds of men and many tons of supplies halfway across the continent, but he had been successful in cooling (if through show-of-force) the fears of the Metis of the Red River Valley. For the present, at least, their culture would not be lost. In addition, the expedition had surely shown American expansionists in Minnesota and elsewhere that the boundary line established in 1783 at the Treaty of Paris between these North American nations would be firmly held.

✶ ✶ ✶

"We heard that there were a few women along, and I told little Johnny here that one of those ladies might just be our sister."

"Oh, Bobby. You still tease as much as ever," Della laughed. But the fact was, she had truly prayed that if there was any possible way she would be reunited with her family.

The two European ladies spent considerable time together in

what they called "sightseeing." This was done during the day when both their husbands were especially busy.

Naturally, Frances wanted all possible time to sketch and Louisa was a most willing companion. Their voyageurs were at their command. So, Della was left with some unspoken-for hours of her own during the day.

It had not been very difficult for a beautiful woman speaking French and enquiring about identical young Metis twins to make her presence in the valley known. But it was the boys who had found her, not vice versa.

"But when will I see Papa?" she kept asking her brothers.

"Papa is in a meeting," or "Papa is with de Lorme," they would tell her.

"But what meeting can be more important than one with his own daughter?" she heard herself whine. She had traveled so far.

Then, before many days, she was in his strong embrace. The four of them were together again. "You could stay, Della." It was the same plea she had heard years before, and she gave the same answer. "Gramma Nell needs me. Except that Mrs. Hopkins and her friend also felt they needed me—which they didn't, really—I would not be away from Gramma right now."

Her father understood. Such separations had been a way of life for him. And the twins finally gave up pleading, though they would not say so in any language but French. "We are French Metis," they said proudly. "No longer Bobby and Johnny, but Dominic and François. We will not beg you to stay!" But they each kissed her sadly when it was time for them to part.

Big Louie, who was as big as always, but now showing a little gray hair along his temples, hugged Della again and again. Unexpectedly he said, "Daughter, I think it may be that we will not meet for a very long time. I see you have worn for me the necklace I gave to you when you became a woman. I hope one day you will have your own daughter to give it to. And I hope you will tell her the story of the canoe and of her voyageur *grandpere*."

Epilogue

Melinda was running in the hallway again, those hard-soled shoes clattering on the shiny wooden floor. She was such an active girl, not unusual for an eight-year-old. In she burst, nearly breathless and smiling ear-to-ear, another Millie, though allowing only her grandmother to call her by that name.

"It's the post, Gramma Dell, and you have one from across the sea." It read:

> To: Mrs. Colin Steven
> 14 Rue St. Dominique
> Montreal, Canada

When the child passed the letter to Della, she asked, "Gramma, why does it have that black mark around the envelope?"

Della rubbed the faded scar in her eyebrow and answered abruptly, "Sit quietly, young Millie, while I read this."

March 11, 1919
London, England

My Dear Della,

Please forgive that this news does not come in my own hand. Sadly, though not unexpectedly, I tell you that my cousin and our friend, Frances Anne Hopkins, has died at the age of eighty-one.

Such family as is nearby attended the service on the coldest of

March days. That included Olive's son and daughter and Manley. You will not be surprised to read that Manley somehow found snowdrops to bring, as he had always done for her birthday. And, I think it is wonderful that all the young ones, even her sisters' children, called her Grandmama.

Many friends from the art associations and from Edward's former circles were also in attendance, though due to my poor eyes, I am not able to name them. My granddaughter, Louisa, who is writing for me, will find a news clipping and send it over next time.

Until I am better able to say more, I remain your friend forever.

Mrs. Alan Scott

Millie

Della held the black-edged page to her heart. She did not realize that tears were sliding down her wrinkled cheeks. When the little girl touched the old woman's arm, Della started and remembered where she was: a sunny window in the home of her youngest son, Andrew Robert Steven.

"Shall I bring Mama, Gramma Dell?" the child asked.

"It's all right now, young Millie. I was only remembering. A long time ago when I was just a little older than you are now, a very special lady came into my life."

"Was she famous, Gramma Dell? Was she a singer? Or a ballerina?"

"No, child. She was an artist. A woman who captured the past and saved it for the future. She was Frances Anne Hopkins."

Afterword

In the period after 1870 Red River was often in the news. The forming of that area, inhabited by North Americans, Metis, Europeans, and Americans into the Province of Manitoba took many painful attempts and many years.

Immediately upon their return to Montreal, Mr. and Mrs. Edward Hopkins departed for England, never to return to the land that had so enchanted them both. Their family continued to grow but only through grandchildren.

Manley Hopkins chose a military career; Raymond ended up living in South Africa where his mother visited at least once. She and Edward had a long and fulfilling retirement living in London and, at last, in the country house he had so longed for.

Frances Anne Hopkins continued to paint for the remainder of her life. She exhibited often and completed commissioned paintings, too, many of these scenes similar to those she had sketched during her twelve years in Canada.

Some of her most famous pictures were huge, wall-sized outdoor scenes. At least seven of these featured canoes and she included her own image, along with her husband, in five of them.

One such painting she presented to her friends Viscount Wolseley and his wife, Lady Louisa. This painting was a long-distance view of Kakabeka Falls, in present day Ontario, just west of Thunder Bay. It depicts the Wolseley Expedition making a difficult portage on the way to Red River.

As was her desire, Frances Anne Hopkins had recorded enough images in her head and in her sketchbooks to keep painting Canadian scenery to the end of her life.

Author's Notes

I am indebted to a number of writers who began the search for Frances Anne Hopkins years ago. Grace Lee Nute, historian and fur trade author, was among the first. Her article "Voyageurs' Artist" appeared in the Hudson's Bay Company publication *The Beaver* in June 1947. Alice M. Johnson published "Edward and Frances Hopkins of Montreal" in that magazine in the Autumn 1971 issue.

Canadian Geographic published "Frances Anne Hopkins: The Lady Who Painted Canoes" by John W. Chalmers, July 1971, and "Rediscovering Voyageur Artist Frances Hopkins," by Margaret Rand, June/July 1982.

The Beaver, Winter 1976, printed an article by Elizabeth Hopkins, daughter of Mrs. Hopkins' stepson, Manley, entitled "Grandmama."

Janet Clark, Guest Curator, and Robert Stacey, Guest Essayist, have published the most recent and most detailed information about this artist's work and life in *Frances Anne Hopkins 1838–1919*, the catalog for a portion of her work on the 1990 tour of four Canadian cities.

Public collections owning original sketchbooks, watercolors, pen and ink drawings, and oils are the Public Archives of Canada in Ottawa, Royal Ontario Museum in Toronto, Glenbow Museum in Calgary, and numerous smaller facilities.

✷ ✷ ✷

Exploring the Fur Trade Routes of North America by Barbara Huck, et al. is an excellent resource for modern-day travelers of the old routes. Maps and award-wining illustrations bring alive the fur trade era.

A Good Solid Comfortable Establishment by Graham MacDonald tells in words and photos the story of Lower Fort Garry, a Hudson's Bay site near Winnipeg. The structure is the only original stone fort still in existence.

Another original stone structure still standing is a church in Lachine, Quebec, now a suburb of Montreal. The story of that church, and to some extent others in the area, is told in *St. Stephen's Church Lachine*, compiled by George Merchant. Governor George Simpson definitely attended this church, though records show that when he disagreed with what was presented in the sermon, he simply marched out of the building. Also recorded is the burial of Annie Ogden Hopkins, Edward's first wife.

And lastly, a portion of the story of British fur-trade explorer David Thompson is told in a very readable version: *Source of the River: Tracking David Thompson Across Western North America*, by Jack Nisbet.

All the above and many other sources were consulted to bring life to the *Canoe Lady*.